TARJEI VESAAS

The Hills Reply

Translated from the Norwegian
by Elizabeth Rokkan

archipelago books

First Archipelago Books edition, 2019

Translated from the Norwegian *Baaten om kvelden*
English translation first published by Peter Owen, 1971
© Gyldendal Norsk Forlag AS, 1968
English translation © Peter Owen and Elizabeth Rokkan, 1971
This edition published by arrangement with Peter Owen Publishers, London.

Library of Congress Cataloging-in-Publication Data
Names: Vesaas, Tarjei, 1897-1970, author. | Rokkan, Elizabeth, translator.
Title: The hills reply / Tarjei Vesaas ;
translated from the Norwegian by Elizabeth Rokkan.
Other titles: Bêaten om kvelden. English
Description: Brooklyn, NY : Archipelago Books, [2019]
Previous edition entitled The boat in the evening.
Identifiers: LCCN 2019000753 | ISBN 9781939810380 (pbk.)
ISBN 9781939810397 (ebook)
Subjects: LCSH: Norway--Fiction.
Classification: LCC PT9088.V6 B313 2019 | DDC 839.823/72--dc23
LC record available at https://lccn.loc.gov/2019000753

Archipelago Books
232 Third Street #A111
Brooklyn, NY 11215
www.archipelagobooks.org

Distributed by Penguin Random House
www.penguinrandomhouse.com

Book design by Megan Mangum. Cover design by Zoe Guttenplan.

This work was made possible by the New York State Council on the Arts
with the support of Governor Andrew M. Cuomo
and the New York State Legislature.

Archipelago Books also gratefully acknowledges the generous support from New York City's
Department of Cultural Affairs, the Nimick Forbesway Foundation, Lannan Foundation,
and the Carl Lesnor Family Foundation.

PRINTED IN THE UNITED STATES OF AMERCIA

The Hills Reply

First Preface

My first dream.
My delicate dream
of gliding water and my dream.

The heart dwells beside gliding rivers.
The rivers eat into the shores.
Shrinking shores lose their name.

There will always be shores
for a dream
of gliding water and my dream.

That waiting time in the serpent's den,
where children stood anxiously, waiting
for the serpent to come out.

Nothing came out
through all the years.
Never out under Man's heel.

A long time ago.
. . . Now it is late,
and the serpent's delicate tracery of bones
gleams in the dark,

hidden between the stones,
plucked clean,
polished in the eternal wind.
Never out under Man's heel.

A wind plays there to nobody,
soundless in the filigreed tracery.
A wind plays past the dark eye.
Eye that stills all activity,
and all thought, and all creeping things,
and the snake in its bitter cursing.

Second Preface

about this fragmentary picture from the loitering boat

The heart is split in two, irresolute between its desires.
Yet the boat has to advance. . . night or day are merely
shifting veils to be traversed. Advance with fierce
courage. Not for the sake of men. For the sake of
insoluble riddles. In utter secrecy
the heart is split in two.

There is movement and life in the boat. One by one,
      pictures appear.
The boat advances with courage that no one understands.
Those on land glimpse the voyage between the sharp
      outlines of shadows.
Much that is unexpected is mingled with it.
Not new things either; they have been there before.

Is *that* what is coming from the banks, the enticing shores
     close by?
Not that . . . just a quick little greeting:
Hey! comes the barely heard call from the shore.
Hey! comes the soft reply from the boat.
That is all.
As if shifting moments existed no more.

Contents

As It Stands in the Memory

THERE HE STANDS in sifting snow. In my thoughts in sifting snow. A father – and his winter-shaggy, brown horse, in snow.

His brown horse and his face. His sharp words. His blue eyes and his beard. The beard with a reddish tinge against the white. Sifting snow. Blind, boundless snow.

Far away, deep in the forest. Sunken roads in the drifts, gullies dug out of the drifts, logging roads walled in by snow.

Blind, boundless forest – because the horizons have disappeared today in the mild, misty snowfall. Here everything is silent, no sound is made on the logging-road in the loose snow as it piles higher and higher.

What is outside?

Nothing, it seems.

There is something outside, but it's a boy's secret, deeply concealed.

He shivers occasionally and glances at the wall of snow

and mist. Of course he knows what ought to be there, but it is easy to imagine very different things when you are a child, or half-child, and too young to be with a sharp-tongued father, among heavy, soaking wet logs and a horse strong as iron.

Why think about what's outside all the time?

Only more snow.

And hillsides that I know out and in, every hollow and cliff.

No use saying that.

I'm here to clear the snow. To make a logging-road.

No use saying that either.

It's not so certain that there is anything outside. During the first hours you spend digging, before you're too tired to think and imagine anything, life starts teeming outside the ring of mist and the wall of snow. Animals crowd round in a ring, their muzzles pointing towards me. Not ordinary animals. Animals I've never seen before. They're as tall as two horses one on top of the other, and they lower red muzzles and strike at the wall of mist while they are thinking. They switch at the snowflakes with long tails, as if it were summer and there were flies. There are so many of them that they can stand side by side in an unbroken ring – and they have small eyes that they almost close as they stand wondering and thinking.

Supposing the snow suddenly stopped falling – would they stand there exposed?

What would they do then?

What will they do anyway?

I want them there, that's what it is.

So there they are. All day long.

Yes, they stand there thinking – while I clear the logging-road, digging and digging and thinking and thinking too. In the snowfall in a blind forest.

The shovel becomes idle in my hands.

Supposing it stopped snowing, supposing they were standing there.

What would they want?

They are so real that they have a slight smell that reaches me. It is probably much stronger close to them, and a little of it reaches me. Perhaps it is not a smell; it is not easy to decide what I sense it with. They stand side by side in a single ring of flesh – but between them and myself there is the wall of mist and the falling snow.

Much too tempting to think about them. The snow collects on their muzzles, and their tails wave, raised as if in fight.

There is a sharp, "What is it?"

The boy starts.

What a question!

What is it? he asks, that one over there with his heavy shovelfuls of snow. An odd question when you can see that splendid ring of strange creatures. What is *he* thinking about over there? Must be thinking about something, he too. But you can't ask him about it.

The question only meant that the shovel had been idle too long. He has a watchful eye for such things, and for many others, that one over there.

This is the toilsome daily round.

The man and the horse have hard tasks. The logs have to be taken the long way through the forest to the river. All the bad weather this winter makes such work endless drudgery.

The stern man gets no answer to his question. But the shovel moves into action again, so all is well. It always goes as that one over there wishes. The gully in the snow has to be opened up farther, to fresh piles of logs lying deep in the snow. There *was* a road here, a gully, but now it is completely wiped out by the storm and the wind. The horse is sent ahead, and he wades through the snow and finds the road again with some delicate instinct of his, then the two of them follow him with their shovels and tramp about, widening the track the horse has made. So it goes, piece by piece.

Endless drudgery.

Don't think about it.

Think about the solid ring of big animals close by in the twilight. Curious creatures that have not been seen in any book.

That's not thinking, it's resting.

Breathe in what must be their smell. Here as everywhere else there is a smell of the hanging weight of fresh moisture. Wet snow, and snow melting on your face.

Restful to think about. Exciting to think about.

EVERYTHING will be gathered here.

The horse, you and I, gathered here.

But we are inside a ring of something no human being has ever seen. He ought to have known it, that one over there. He of the few and sharp words.

There, he has stopped shoveling.

What is he doing? He's leaning on the snow shovel, staring straight in front of him.

It was quiet before, yet it seems as if he has only become so this minute. He is not leaning on the shovel because he is tired, not so early in the day. It must be something else.

He is looking at something.

He too.

No sound now. The slight noise of the shoveling has stopped. The horse is standing in the snowdrift tearing strips of bark off a birch sapling with his teeth, but that makes no sound either. The horse is wet high up on his flanks from the wading. There the moisture from the driving snow meets the dripping blanket he has on his back. He is wet all over. He looks at the two of them with his gentle, fathomless eyes, stops stripping the bark and simply stands still. You can see he's thinking.

There are three of us.

We are thinking, all three of us.

What are we thinking?

Out of something. Perhaps out of this.

Yes. Out of this.

This never-ending weather. The snowflakes fluttering down in a senseless dance, settling on the horse's back, on father's shoulders, on everything that provides room. They dance as if in fury, determined to fill all the gullies, and today's work may yet again be wasted by tomorrow. Out of this.

Might as well switch off the ring of animals and get out – since father's standing like that.

Look at him.

A few tense minutes.

Father is dreaming a secret dream. It's unbelievable.

No, it's not unbelievable. One has heard one thing and another down the years.

Perhaps I know what he's dreaming about. Sometimes

he's said things that gave the rest of us an inkling of it, and a twinge of conscience – because he was so hopelessly far from his dream, a dream that would never come true.

I expect that's where he is now.

He has wandered there in the middle of this snowfall, during this exhausting shoveling. These stupidly heavy logs that have to be lifted, lifted by a bad back. He looks strong, but once he overtaxed his strength and will never mend. He is not strong – he has that build because he *was* strong once upon a time.

Perhaps he was not strong then either? But they say he was.

These are good, exciting moments. Nothing is moving except for the dancing snowflakes. The horse listens, his head turned away from the driving snow. Are we going to stand like this for a long time without moving?

Then they would perhaps start to move in from their ring and run among us with their muzzles and their tails, and all the tails would stand straight up in the air.

What would they do?

Do they eat creatures like us? In the twinkling of an eye?
No, no. They don't eat anyone.

They can laugh. They would stick up their tails in the air and laugh.

Hush…

A start goes through the tableau. He gives it a start, that man over there. Out of his dream.

A quick, keen glance this way. No, nobody's going to be allowed to stand idle too long.

Was there perhaps a slightly ashamed expression in the eye too? But the movement continues. He grips the snow shovel, and drives it into the drift.

The one who doesn't see anything, or doesn't bother about what he sees, is the brown horse. He doesn't bat an eyelid.

The horse, yes.

Is *this* what he's thinking?

SNOWBOUND, snowed under, and trapped in the snow.
    This is my song and thus is my song,
    the day is long

and this is my song,
let me simply get snowbound and trapped in the snow.
The day is long, and the day is long.
It is good to sleep, snowbound and trapped in the snow.

THE HORSE, yes. It happens to be the horse's turn.

He has to go ahead, wade into the snow, and find another piece of the road. The man comes out of his dream to set him in motion. He seizes the reins.

He does not look at his big boy. He seems to be embarrassed about something.

"H'up, Brownie."

The horse looks ahead, his eyes are fathomless. The snow sprinkles over him, melting on the wet, warm blanket on his back.

The man guides the horse in the right direction. The patient horse does not falter, but throws himself into it, leaning against the drift, wading and trampling a passage for himself. They have no sled with them today; the horse must move freely if he is to get through this.

He manages a few feet, then has to stop to get his breath. His master understands this. He turns the horse, and they go back to the big boy who has begun shoveling. The horse, half swimming in the snow, arrives back on the cleared road. There he is allowed to stand and tear at the birch twigs with his teeth, and perhaps sing his song somewhere deep inside himself, in an unknown world where human beings have no business intruding.

The man seizes the shovel.

The big boy shovels.

The big boy stands inside his ring of wild animals, shoveling snow.

Who is singing?

The horse is singing his song somewhere deep inside himself, and the man and the boy are dreaming their dreams. It has to be. The potent melody that the boy feels is coming in waves from his secret ring is another matter. He hears it as he shovels until his arms grow stiff.

The weather is improving, the snow stops falling. They can see a little farther, but still into the mist.

I'd rather the mist didn't disappear. I don't want to look over to long ridges and hillsides, and even farther, just now. They must be gathered here. I am too young for this – if I were to look across to all the mountain tops I would lose courage altogether. I must have that strange, secret ring just outside.

There they are standing side by side, and this fact turns to strength in him, lending power to his arm. He tries to turn his image of them into a kind of defiance, to turn it into shovelfuls of snow. They call out something that has this effect. They raise their muzzles as they do so.

It is not a beautiful sound, but it is a sound for the perplexed young boy shoveling snow. He does not know what it is, but it will become stronger later, stronger than now – for it is not now, it is not now.

Shut in by walls of snow on a blind and mute mid-winter's day. The child watches his father. His father lifts huge, heavy lumps of snow with his shovel. He is steaming with sweat. His face is again severe, closed. It is like hearing a word of gratitude to recall the moment just now when he, too, was resting on his shovel and thinking about something that was certainly not in this place, and that was restful to him.

They do not exchange a word now.

They do not look at each other. In turn each starts in surprise to see that the other is watching him. Something hidden is gathered here, of which they are unaware. This does not mean anything – yet it means so much that it makes one double up.

THE MAN takes out his watch. The child pays careful attention. Perhaps it is time for a break?

It is. It does not have to be mentioned – since as little as possible should be spoken about. He can see it is time for a break by the way father put the big, silver turnip away in his pocket.

Almost nothing need be said when you have eyes, and when you have your own song.

The break has been in the forefront of their minds for a good while. And it comes punctually. The fir-tree is standing ready to receive them, a tree all hanging, wide-spreading branches; with the help of the snow a house has formed beneath it. The man sees to the horse. Green, fragrant hay. His son coaxes a flame on the hearth quickly assembled out of three stones, and puts the kettle on. Neither of them has said a word. The horse munches hay. It is pleasant to listen to in the snow; more expressive than any speech. It is as if they are sending one another pleasant messages by means of the only sound in existence.

The fire warms up and crackles. The kettle boils. They munch cold sandwiches mixed with hot liquid and with steam from their wet clothes. The warmth enters their bodies and their sight grows blurred.

The man's eyes are dim, he is staring inwardly at something. The child is strangely struck, almost scared to see the stern man staring into something far beyond the present. The child is frighteningly alone.

Where is the wordless man wandering, this man who is not wordless when he's with the right people? The sight of him makes the boy forget his childish ring of animals. What is he thinking about at this moment? It's not about the people at home – he's sure of that.

The child ponders this anxiously. And then the question is blurted out. The same question given back from earlier today:

"What is it?"

Without meaning to, it sounds frightened.

The man gives a start.

"Is anything the matter, then?" he says quite sharply. His tireless manner of dealing with unwelcome questions.

"No," mumbles the child hastily.

The child withdraws again. He has a guilty conscience, that's the trouble. Because he always sides with the quiet, strong partner at home, is always on her side when something is the matter – and therefore seems to be against this man of few words – who is not at all a man of few words, who is made welcome and makes people laugh as soon, and as quickly, as he likes.

But *here* there is no one to be happy with, to talk to about horses. The child knows all this far too well. On especially exhausting or boring workdays the man takes on the expression he has now. He stares out into something one dare not ask him about.

He is lonely, and I am lonely – and she who is at home and so very different, what is she? Yet they talk to each other just the same, about many things.

The one who is least lonely here is the horse.

No, no.

The warmth has found its way in. The food and the warmth and the work are all having their effects on the man. He nods and drowses.

The child watches him intently while he is asleep. He cannot discover anything.

He's dreaming about something now.

What can it be?

What is reflected in his face? There is life in it as he sleeps.

ARE THEY FOND of each other?

Yes! Many signs of that.

But strangers to each other.

Don't know.

SO VERY BRIEF – his eyes are open already and looking around in confusion. A quick movement to take his watch out of his pocket.

"Oh!" he exclaims in amazement and puts his ear to the watch, to see if it has stopped.

The child has a desire to call to him: Do you think you've been dreaming as long as that? But he cannot bring out a word on this occasion either.

The horse is not munching, only half-dozing.

"My word, this will never do," says the man, in rebuke to someone, and gets to his feet.

His eyes are still distant. He is not here. He puts the bit into the horse's mouth. The horse opens his lips slightly to make room.

THEY HAVE FINISHED that section and the horse is set to trampling down a new piece. He knows what he is supposed to do; all that's necessary is to take hold of the reign with scarcely a word.

"H'up, Brownie."

But something is said to him, at least, so that he will feel they are working together, that there are three of them. He wades, darkening with the wet, is given breathing space, tears at a piece of birch bark, and wades on ahead again.

Using all his strength.

The only one who has any strength.

His steel-shod hooves trample erratically in the deep snow. It is difficult to control his feet in it. He tramples and wades, determined to go forward. A long, long time until supper – and thus is my song.

What was that now?

Was it a sound?

No sound, but something has happened. Something red on the lumps of snow tossed up by the struggling horse's hooves. Blood on the lumps of snow.

Not a sound. No pause either.

But this man turns the horse in a flash, so that he wades the short distance back again. The child gets out of the way, knowing what this is.

"Has he kicked himself?"

"Obviously."

Shortly after: "He's kicked himself badly."

The man cautiously strokes the bloodied snow away from the horse's foot. There is a long red weal in the leg just above the hoof. The shining sharp shoe on the other hoof trod in the wrong place. Cut by his own shoe. Dirty melting snow trickles down the leg into the wound.

Dumbly hurting.

The horse droops his head as if dreaming, takes his weight off the leg, then droops lower. He is with man, with man in good and evil times. Has given himself over to man.

HIS STERN MASTER is hurriedly searching his memory. He does not see his staring child, but looks back into distant times, searching for the threads of experience. Never be at a loss. Don't stand uncertain in the desert places and the blizzard. No man must do that.

Centuries of life with horses and snow. Lore from father to son. Harmful or wise. Inherited down the ages.

Advice about accidents, when far away from any first aid: Use whatever means you have, quickly and firmly. A cold breath from far back in time: Cleanse the warm wound with your own salt water. It has been done since heathen times. Whether it helped or hindered nobody knows.

So the stern man kneels beside the horse's hoof, fumbles with his wet clothes and makes himself ready.

An echo from heathen times, unknown to the half-grown child. The child is ignorant of what it knows.

THE BIG BOY watches, embarrassed. Why embarrassed? He does not know. He does not know about this, there has never been any need for it. He sees his father making himself ready, sees the horse leaning forward, sees his father fumbling nervously.

No washing of the wound. Nothing at all. He has nothing to offer.

His father, never one to fail, flushes. He raises his voice, as if in pain, turning to the child.

"I've been sweating too much today."

As if this defeat is the child's fault – that's what it sounds like, the child senses danger. Wants to get away. It is much too late.

No, I won't.

Too late.

His voice chops the air: "Come on, you try! What are you waiting for?"

THE EMBARRASSED CHILD is drawn into it, into blind, dark rings. Swelling, incomprehensible opposition, helpless opposition when it is precisely help he must offer.

I can't do this.

Why not?

A thought shoots far out to one side, out towards the

ring of mist, out to the big creatures standing there with red muzzles and lifted tails and small eyes – standing there making *their* hidden ring.

He thinks of them as a help.

But they make no move. He is and remains utterly alone. With wild courage he stammers to his father: "What about you, then?"

Although he saw his father's failure well enough, he manages to say it in defiance, stammering inside the walls of snow.

But what's to be done besides stammering it to this wall of rock and then giving in?

"YOU HEARD ME," he says, still on his knees at the horse's feet.

His tone is harsh. The distant echoes from heathen times thunder in his voice, making it like this, turning it to stone.

The boy answers instantly: "Yes, I heard you."

"Then come *along*!"

"All right."

WHY SHOULD IT SEEM so difficult? It ought to be simple, surely, to give help to the lamed horse?

The things you *must* do are usually possible.

The impossible becomes real when you must.

The impossible does not exist when you must.

Anyone who knows so many secrets, who knows about the ring of animals, ought to be ashamed of himself.

Yes, he is ashamed too, and comes wading across to the horse and his father. Burning, he kneels down and makes himself ready.

There are three of them. There is nobody else. But all the same this is happening within the ring of animals, which only one of the three knows about.

Close to the horse's hoof.

The horse droops his head as if dreaming about something, but it is the hurt and the throbbing that make the dumb animal behave this way. He lifts his hoof, standing on three legs, lifts his hoof high enough to raise the wound above the cold snow they are all standing in.

The horse, large and helpless. Strong and utterly helpless,

but together with man, trusting man in his hurt. Perhaps trusting completely in the unfledged being down in the snow beside the wound.

Large or small, man must come to a painful wound.

This is my song.

EMBARRASSED AND TREMBLING beside the horse's hoof.

He wants to do as he is told, but cannot do a thing. He knows beforehand that he cannot, but he must pretend he can. He has a curious sensation: what seemed to be a dark wall opening – and his father stepping out of it to speak words of stone to his child. Stepping straight out of a black wall with strange advice that he himself could not follow.

He failed himself, and turned his failure into words of stone to the frightened child. He stepped out of the stone wall like a barking dog, so that everything is doomed to failure.

No use, in spite of centuries-old lore. Horse and man in

isolation must help themselves when in pain. Old, black lore straight out of the wall. You cannot follow it when you are a child.

This stern man has inherited it from down the centuries, and stands self-possessed, giving orders, beside his own defeat. He demands curtly, "Get on with it."

BITTER MOMENTS. The child can do nothing either.

He could have called to his father: Haven't I sweated just as much as you today? And it would have been true, and reason enough.

But he is silent for a different reason, one that goes deeper.

The black command that came out of the wall of stone. It cannot be explained. He cannot perform. Not one miserable drop.

A caustic look from the man above him rests on him and paralyzes him so that he cannot move either. But nothing will come of this anyhow; the man's caustic eye saw this in an instant.

Miserably the child kneels in the snow beside the horse's

raised, smarting leg. The steel shoe glistens on his hoof from the trickling blood on the polished metal.

Go on, shout out loud, he says to himself. Shout at him that he was no better. He was just as hopeless.

No.

You don't shout such things out loud at a man such as this. You keep silent instead.

Nothing but embarrassment within the wall of mist. Let me shout about something else that's hidden from you, then: about the thousands of creatures who are switching their tails and standing so close together that the warmth passes from one to another. The creatures with their searching, uplifted muzzles. *They* will come running if I shout – because they are mine. There are so many of them that it would grow dark in the wood as if it were evening.

Stupid thoughts flashing past. There are only three of them here. Only three, even if he were to shout until he burst.

But he cannot for the life of him manage to wash the wound in this doubtful manner. He regains his power of movement and is already getting to his feet.

Once on his feet he sees unjust anger flushing in the face before him. With slight ceremony he is pushed aside, his own cheeks burning with shame.

Not a word.

It is a double defeat.

Nothing for it but to fumble with his stiff, snow-sodden clothes again.

The horse droops his head and appears to have noticed nothing, as he keeps his leg raised, a helpless creature together with helpless man, dumb for thousands of years with man.

NOT A WORD.

The stern man with his secret, gentle dream, what about him?

He tears of his jacket, tears off his shirt, jerkily, with angry gestures. The defeat seems to have turned into anger. He rips his shirt with a screech of the cloth, winds it around the wounded limb and knots it together. Not a word the whole time. He must try to keep the cold snow out of the open wound, and it is a long way home. A long way in the loose snow; it has not had time to harden in the gully. Home to see the horse as quick as they can.

Three of them equally silent, on the way home.

The dirty wound bleeds in their consciences, whether with reason or not.

The big boy bears the hurt. He will remember this to the end of his life.

No, the horse bears the hurt, but there is a difference. His smart is pure and honest.

What will the man remember? The child knows nothing about that. He does not know anything about him for certain. But he was dreaming over his shovel; that is all he knows.

THE SNOW STARTS to fall again. The mist thickens.

And the ring of animals?

At this moment the whole ring of animals vanishes. They cannot be kept back. No use calling them. They will not be conjured up again.

The big boy bears the hurt instead, a shapeless burden, but one that will settle for good.

The horse bears the *burning* hurt.
Without a sound, like the others.

> I am with man,
> and no other than man.
> I am with man
> all the day long.
> I am the horse,
> and this is my song.

In the Marshes and on the Earth

A HUGE, BARE MARSH.

What am I doing here, out of doors so early?

I shall go. To see. Just to see.

Here too.

Early morning on a big marsh. I go in perplexity, to search for something important. Why should anyone do that? For reasons that seem decisive to oneself. But reasons that one does not wish to examine too closely.

There is no need to ask: Do I really see this? This is obviously a black marsh early in spring before it has turned green, and early in the morning when the air is full of the taste of ice. The snow was lying here only recently.

It feels as if there is black earth with icy snow patches inside oneself on a morning like this. That is why one goes out wandering.

It feels like that when something is wrong. Nothing you can point to, but wrong all the same.

Lurch out of a house. Lurch your way out to a marsh.

I am too young.

But everything is so marvellously wrong. It's so horribly exciting.

Then you have arrived at the marshes.

Chilly and early. The moss barely escaped being stiffened with frost last night.

BLACK, NAKED AND WIDE. Late spring. There can't be much use in walking here either when you have lost your footing. You can at any rate pretend it is so, and lose your footing for an instant, no longer. You must go and find something while you are in the void, and when you see a marsh as wide and as bare as this one, which you watched as it hid itself in the spring night yesterday evening, you have to walk out on it the next morning as soon as it is daylight.

Mist has been resting on the marsh during the night. Now it is dissolving into restless skeins. Many of them have moved away, others are still lying about lazily – the remnants of the events of the night, a cold, raw spring night, with its awakening life.

The light comes earlier each morning. There are clear, strict laws of life in such a marsh. One must go out of it. There must be something worth finding.

Always something one must find, though ignorant of what is going on. If only it had had a suitable name, this strange lack one cannot shake off.

If it had had a name it would have been smaller and less aggressive. Then one could have gone straight up to it to see whether it really was anything important.

My body gives a shudder. Am I being watched from somewhere along the edge of the marsh? Sheer fancy. I think so because I am as naked as the marsh.

But the feeling persists.

Someone is watching from the edge of the marsh. It's that curious tingling you get.

And there! – a grating noise in the crusted snow. A few patches of crust are left, over there between the trees. So there was someone there after all. My ears are keen and hear well.

Is someone leaving this place? One's eyes are keen too, when one is experiencing this nameless pull, but there is nothing to be seen. Only the grating footsteps. It must be someone who has been longing to walk on the snow crust, and is looking for the last remaining patches. Now he's moving away without revealing himself.

I don't like that sort of thing. People shouldn't go creeping about among the trees when one is in the grip of the pulling sensation, naked on a black marsh. No one is to walk among the trees watching me.

Grey or dun-colored tussocks, with last year's pale straws flattened by the weight of this winter's snow. Many creatures have been trampling here, and in the hollow left by each foot there is a tiny puddle. As if the marsh had been given a thousand eyes. Blurred eyes that are sightlessly still or which look indifferently out, utterly strange and all alike. The marsh is still dead; the summer with its whirring life has not yet awoken, seems not yet conceived.

It is right to walk here, but one is hard put to know why one does so.

Am I dreaming this?

Am I not walking here at all?

How shall I really find out?

Let's affirm that I am walking here, that everything I see and feel is real.

The marsh is unknown to me, and yet it seems familiar. It seems as if I have walked here day after day, and nothing has happened. Yesterday evening I came here and watched the night settling out on the marsh – and yet I feel as though I have been walking here endlessly. Is that when things happen – at night? One must find out something, to pull oneself upright.

Some of the countless eyes in the marsh seem to focus and look at me. The thought is not unwelcome; it is as if a link has been made, a tiny floating link between myself and what is here. It is important. One must gradually learn the truth about the boundaries between what is great and what is small.

MORE GRATING over there in the invisible snow crust. Why is he over there moving about? Why didn't he clear off? It's not his time any longer, it's morning. One cannot help being shocked by it, although the snow crust is among one's favorite childhood memories.

Just let him go.

This marsh is enormously wide. The edges have disappeared for the most part in drifting morning mist. It is quite noiseless, except for those grating footsteps, and now he has gone for today, I hurriedly decide.

We shall never meet.

AT THE SAME INSTANT: a darkness in the air.

Not completely dark: a mighty bird sweeps past just above my head and wheels round to land far away on the marsh.

That too.

Is the great crane *here*?

Do the cranes come here?

The first thing to do is to throw oneself flat on the ground, and try to make oneself invisible among the low-growing tussocks and bushes; to make this shy giant, the crane, think one has vanished. To hide one's human face from the distant voyager, the shy bird that has come home. To bore one's chin and mouth down into the moss until only the eyes are showing. For with one's eyes one may mirror the shy, pure crane.

The moss with its taste of what has been or what shall be – it is on one's lips, it is the crown of the marsh. Enormous objects exist down in the marsh-darkness and the marsh-horrors – but up in the light of day there is only the moss, delicate and innocent on the summit.

That was the crane arriving.

It mistrusts man.

There are probably more of them, if one has come. Another wheels in and settles.

Of course. They come in flocks. I've probably stumbled on their own marsh, in trying to find an old marsh-dream, or whatever it is I'm looking for. The cranes have come to spend the summer here, to raise their young, this year as last year.

Shy, shy – they float down far away. In a flash they saw there was something that did not belong here. The powerful wingspan seemed to clutch the air. Better to settle far away. They mistrust the object lying in the marsh. But neither will they give up their own marsh.

A darkness in the air. Was it a shock? No, they are welcome. I didn't know about them, but they are welcome all the same. They are a part of what once is circling round, wishing to approach, wishing to fill a void with. Welcome with all that they are.

The great bird folds his wings. With my eyes above the moss I can watch. It stands in the marsh with an uplifted, inquiring head. The next one follows immediately after and takes up the same position. I am quivering with excitement; it is like a kind of happiness. I am lying in cold marsh moisture, that slowly penetrates my clothes, making me damp and filthy, but I am warmed by the sight of the cranes. I am on the cranes' own territory; I seem to have entered a sacred place where one has no right to be.

In any case it is essential to press myself down into the moss and make myself as invisible as I can. To become a pale tussock in a windcheater beside the dwarf birch bushes. To stare blindly, as the hundreds of puddles are doing. To convince myself that the birds will be taken in by it.

To stare at the cranes. That's a lot in itself. One after the other arcs down. Are they surprised about something? The spring must be colder and more naked than they had imagined when they set out.

No one told them about it; they had to make their journey without knowing how things looked on their marsh. They obeyed a sound within themselves, and left. Now they are standing here, somewhat doubtful in a frozen spring.

Wave after wave of joy passes through me, in spite of the penetrating moisture that is trying to disturb my happiness. The air is continually darkened with wings. They settle down at a distance, long-necked, searching, on guard. My marsh eye watches them and can mirror them.

The crane's eye also seems to rest on everything. From

the air they saw the windcheater tussock that should not have been there. They move far away and look in that direction.

Come closer! I wish at the same moment, as intensely as never before.

They do not understand. It does not occur to them to approach a human being. They have returned from a long journey. They walk, dignified and cautious, far away and without apprehension. The human means nothing to them.

But how must this end? And what is really happening to me?

They walk there in the serene ferment after their long journey. They stretch their necks, manoeuvring in order to settle down and rest in familiar surroundings. In equal ferment, the bundle lies among the tussocks, following their movements.

This must end in something special from the way they're moving. They don't seem to be settling down yet, after all.

Fresh stab of joy. It's sure to end in the dance I've heard about. The dance will soon begin.

Now that they have arrived after their great journey, and their mysterious experiences, the dance will break free. They have reached their goal in the land of snow.

AND BEFORE one is prepared for this rare sight, it happens.

The crane is dancing.

The marsh has acquired a new content, a hidden magnitude brought by the crane. The marsh has been lying here, knowing about it all winter. The crane is dancing now.

LOOK AT IT ONCE, and then never again.

The crane is dancing. Look at it once and for all.

The cold marsh moisture penetrates my clothes and my skin.

My position is cramped, making many muscles ache or sleep – but I scarcely feel it, it is not important, I think only of concealing as much of myself as possible.

How long have I been lying without moving and become

one with marsh moisture and marsh cold and with all the puddles around me? I don't know.

It is not relevant. One does not inquire about time or moisture. The cranes began dancing.

Something broke out in them, together with the spring, and broke out as dance with extraordinary gestures and strange exaggerations.

They are certainly not thinking as clearly now as when they came sweeping in over the land. Their sight is not as keen. In the fever of the dance they are moving gradually in my direction. They are much closer than before – in their stiff, solemn, yet harrowing dance. Blinded by the dance they do not see the strange tussock. Still for some reason moving in this direction.

Soon they will be close beside me.

Oh no, it won't happen – the ritual will not make them so blind as to trample on me. But gradually I am among them all the same. That's the effect they have on me.

Come closer, I wish in my delirium.

It is a strong wish. Stronger than necessary perhaps, if this were observed from the outside, but extremely important to me in the moss.

They dance and mime, and it is important. Their curious writings in the ritual seem to become extremely important to me too. Come closer.

They come closer as the pace quickens, but not on account of me and *my* delirium. Perhaps there is something about their movements that causes it, that guides them.

AGAIN ONE HAS TO ASK: Do I see this? Or have I fallen deep into a marsh-dream?

Is it mirrored in all these blurred marsh eyes round about, as in mine?

One has to ask: Who is this, dancing and gesticulating? Do I see it?

Crane after crane – what does it mean?

It could have been a dream, it is true. But it is no dream. I am lying in the marsh all wet and I know that it is real. I might be bewitched of course.

Birds, one says, facilely. They are a heavenly throng. This is more than mere birds. Far more than what one sees when not bewitched. Someone has bewitched me and the marsh and all the puddles.

This is beyond my concerns. I only feel that it is so. I see it mirrored and feel it once more, even though it is beyond my concerns. The great birds were ecstatic and bewitched when they arrived, and they sweep all else with them.

The ritual will be played out in the guise of a bird.

But it is still beyond me. There is savagery and frenzy in their stiff, dignified cross-turns and inventive gestures. Something chilled and harrowed and solemn. Some sort of suppressed and yet uncontrollable sound must guide the antics that are released and re-captured themselves with a crosswise motion. They are not birds, they are *ourselves* when we have passed between the millstones, crossed the thorny wastes, gone through the fire, undertaken wondrous journeys and given away our hearts to things unworthy of it – with the resulting humiliation unto death.

Then it happens.

Then we must dance like this. Then we clothe ourselves in the proud guise of the crane and sail through the world, away from the fleshpots, to find a familiar marsh, utter wild shrieks and invent frenzied gestures.

IN ALL THIS the puddles, too, act out their ritual. Between the small ones that have formed in animal tracks there are large puddles and pools around a brook that has wandered out on to the marsh and is finding it difficult to escape. There are deep pools, with swaying, half floating turves. In this water one sees the dance when it spreads out to the banks. Someone lying with his chin in the moss can catch only glimpses of it, but he does see it: the dance in the water-mirror, head down and feet up, making it even more real and true.

THE WEAK BANKS give way under the weight of the enormous birds. They move right out among the broken stalks of last year's withered grasses that dip their heads in the water. The turves shiver delicately. The water shivers in rhythm, and the ripples shatter the mirror image. But not for long. The surface is smoothed out, the image returns; it all shivers anew, it all moves in rhythm and all is solemn frenzy.

On floating turves the dance now glides suddenly away from me. They throw themselves backwards so that they seem to crash on the bottom of the marsh at the bottom of the water. None of them are afraid, but all show signs of what looks like extreme anxiety. Not because of the human being; they cannot see him. From the dance it appears that they have frost at the core and fever in the blood. All of them have doubly displayed their ritual and their hearts' core; as for the one who sees the end – head up or down, it will be all the same to him.

But the end has not yet come, I exclaim soundlessly, down in the moss. They have plenty of strength left.

An excess of strength, sweep of wings and flight across

country after country. Yet there is stamina left for this power-squandering spectacle, even upside down.

Dance! I beg, agitated and silent, from where I lie, my extremities numb. Dance! I must see how it ends.

An end I scarcely dare contemplate.

Within my numb exterior there is a turmoil almost in step with the dance of the cranes. The dance has taken possession of me. I am unable to see the puddles like eyes in the marsh, but I know how indifferently they blink. My own eyes burn. This is torture as well as excitement. Torture to hold out without stirring. So one throws oneself as best one can into a muffled echo of the cranes' frenzy. If only one could share their movement and shrieking, shriek with the shrieking birds, about what one wishes to know!

I dare not. They would be gone before I was halfway to my knees.

Dance, I beg them – because I seem to have been able to echo their fever, so that it feels as if I am shouting my message aloud when the birds shriek theirs. There is no sound really. If I were to try to imitate the shriek of the cranes the huge birds would stand as if turned to stone and then disappear into the clouds.

The sky would darken with mighty wings in broad daylight. Perhaps they would never come back.

Or perhaps they would attack me, the whole flock, and torture me. There are so many of them, they have the strength to do it. Oh no, not that!

But perhaps I would remain here as perplexed as ever after being able to call out, after giving vent to a burden borne for a long time.

They had better dance instead.

Dance, I beg them. They are not the only ones who are liberating themselves from their burdens; it is of equal concern to me.

BUT IS THAT IT? Liberation for someone?

Liberation is a big word. It doesn't suit me; what am I to be liberated from? On the contrary, I must be able to receive. To fill a void.

One deludes oneself daily.

I felt achingly hollow and destitute when I came this way over the marsh in the morning chill. What is it that glimmers now? Is it something for that void?

There is still movement.

As long as the dance lasts.

The difficult knot will not loosen; it has not been torn apart by the pressure. That is not why the cranes are dancing in any case. They are not dancing it away, they are showing it to one another. One cannot see through the tangles anywhere. Not yet.

Part of oneself lying numb in the moisture, feeling stabs of heat elsewhere, burning with impatience.

Must I find out more?

About what?

Oh, there are so many things.

The cranes intensify this feeling. One can always find out more. As long as the mirrored head or the upright head is above the surface. As long as one manages to travel across floating, shivering tussocks one can find out more.

From these bewitched birds one can find out more.

IF ONLY ONE could give them a message about this, telling them to dance more and to dance differently. Very differently. They look as if they can do it.

With my chin buried in the moss I wish to the nearest one that is rising and falling: Come closer. Come close.

Boldly they reveal themselves in the dance. They reveal their harrowed and astonished bird minds so that one is in no doubt. Come closer.

They do not immediately obey my intense wish. There was not enough force behind it for that. They are moving on hanging tussocks, feeling the ground give way and urge them on to more frenzied gestures. If they were to drift over here, it is not likely to be on account of my intense wish.

But a stream of wishes is directed at them from the boy with his face half buried in the marsh. The sight of them makes one confused. No one can shout and no one can sing with his mouth in the marsh, but some kind of intuitive contact has been made all the same.

They come closer. The nearest one is not so very far away.

Several of them have paused, their heads lifted high on their long necks, looking inquiringly about them. Sharp-eyed as they are, they must have noticed the object in the moss again.

Does he no longer startle them? He can well believe it might be so.

Are they coming here?

No, they are turning away.

Nothing to bother about, on their wild, joyous day. They are still possessed by the dance.

But the nearest one seems curious all the same. It intends to come this way, stepping tentatively on the thin tussocks. It moves gradually in this direction, its head lifted high.

Another one notices this, and follows, cautiously and a little anxiously.

All the others resume the dance. Some of them have not even paused. Only these two are still looking this way.

Shall I call to it?

No, it would be gone at once.

As it is, they are approaching through the stagnant

puddles. The birds are walking towards this strange object in the marsh that they noticed a long time ago, that does not move, that they are inquisitive about, and that does not threaten them.

They pause a short distance away. They were born shy. Heads higher than ever.

This is the spot; they will not come closer. But they are really very close; I can see right into their eyes. Then one stops whispering wishes, they might notice. Just concentrate on the nearest one, that one that really did come of its own accord.

A feeling comes over me that now there are nothing but eyes above the marsh. A thought creeps in, how extraordinary this must look: a pair of eyes sticking up out of the moss like two stalks – and nothing more.

Nothing is moving at this spot now. All movement is over there, here it has petrified. How far from me are they? Five or six paces. Right beside me.

I certainly shan't beg them to come closer now. The proud head is lifted high on guard, a beam of light strikes straight out of the eye that is turned towards me. Straight towards me without blinking, and thus we are petrified.

DO I KNOW WHAT is coming from that wide-open eye? No. It could be anything at all; it could very well be fear. No, it is not fear. The bird may have been shy, but it has overcome that now. One can probably read surprise in it, surprise at anything strange. Is there any kind of understanding? No.

Desperately I latch on to the remote possibility that some kind of understanding is radiating from the bird after all. We understood each other completely during the dance.

Nonsense!

But I so desperately want it to be understanding. A proud, alien bird – does anyone know all that may reside in it?

I look it straight in the eye. I look at its tall elegance. It looks at my stalk-eyes in the moss.

At last the bird does something: it turns and looks at me from a slightly different direction.

The enormous wings are at rest alongside its body. One thinks of its wing span as a resting wind, always ready.

It is the eye that rivets me. I am sure it is asking me certain questions. But mine are probably asking more. My smarting eyes that are sticking out of the moss on stalks.

But I have seen the dance of the cranes, I say to the searching, slightly arrogant eye. What did I not see there? I ask uselessly. The eye is so clear, and utterly superior. No one saw how it was during the dance.

The crane does not stir. Now the other also approaches stepping high, and pauses beside the first. Both of them equally close to the creature in the moss and the wind-cheater.

They are equally tall. Each turns one eye towards me, full of light.

But they have no explanation to give me. That was something I invented in my perplexity. They do not help me. They are big and secure and shy. Yet the disquieting dance is within them, ready to be unleashed. The dance that still continues over there on the marsh.

The dance that it was so easy to share.

Their eyes are tranquil lights resting on me, without any message.

Come closer, I beg them once more, from somewhere deep within me. I am lying in the wet marsh. My heart is pounding against the raw tussocks. It is good and painful, both at the same time.

They still seem to think they are close enough, standing in their wonderment or whatever it may be. I do not move a muscle, do not lift my face, am nothing but protruding eyes. They are not afraid, but they are careful to have their wings open ready, just in case. I can't help wondering if they have a line of communication open to me? I can only hope that it is so. An open channel, where we can search for the mystery we share while we walk in the marshes and on the earth.

The light in the eye is without expression, I now decide. But then I start, for they suddenly take a few paces towards me, and have come so close that I could seize the long, sinewy leg of the bird if I stretched out my arm.

I do not attempt it. There was a hint of unfriendliness in their movements. Again I cannot help thinking that they could easily put an end to me on the spot if they wished. If they were to begin, the entire savage flock would storm in this direction. If these two were to shriek a warning to the others it would be over in a moment.

They must not come closer, for then they would trample on me. They do not. I am lying stock-still as if lifeless.

But I have seen something, seen them in their naked dance – and I manage to stare at them fixedly, trying to keep looking into their eyes. If I were to look down they would perhaps attack, since the change from wonderment to hostility occurred so quickly.

They must not come closer. Nor must they give warning. Their shriek is horrible and can start a chain reaction in the others. And yet – I want them here, even though my body is tortured and freezing. I say behind my closed mouth: Please. Don't go. Don't go for a long time. I must see it all. Don't go. Do something that will frighten me, if you like, but don't go.

As if in answer to this the second bird makes a leap into the air, is airborne and fans its wings wide. Huge. Buoyant. All is air and movement and freedom. It has been wheeling above rushing rows of countries. It is probably only doing this because it is tired of standing still; it will not take off for good. And it settles at once and becomes as still as before.

The first one stands watching me in the same position. It is becoming a struggle to have that unmoving eye on me, feeling as if I have to answer it the whole time. Soon I shan't know what to do.

The marsh has a painful grip on me. I am soaking wet and feel heavy as a stone. The thoughts that woke during our dance – about knots that would unravel and be illuminated – can no longer be sustained. The huge pair of wings that gave their display – they raised my spirits a little, but not enough, not even enough to get my chin up out of the moss. What are they going to do now?

Having shown me what wings and air are, they stand in silent inspection. I can hold out no longer; I must do something, no matter what.

AND YET I AM STILL wishing, Stay! as I know that this must come to an end.

What am I thinking of? Haven't I been able to share in far more than I could ever have imagined?

But I can see that we are no longer speaking to each other in any way. They are merely inspecting me with their round bird eyes. Mine are beginning to swim. I cannot hold out. Something must be done at once. There is a long crane's foot within an arm's length – they must have edged even closer – and I shoot up out of the moss, becoming more than two eyes, throw out an arm and seize the hard, tall stalk of a leg – and at last I shriek my own shriek at this unyielding enigma.

The shriek must have been lying in my throat all the time; it came of itself.

The effect follows like lighting.

The bird starts on being seized by the leg, and shrieks a reply to my shriek before it has died away – a horrible sound. Like lightning it strikes at me with its giant beak, slashing a strip of fire down my face in its haste.

I lie prone, expecting to be slashed again. It makes its departing leap, easily jerking itself away from my half-hearted grip, becomes airborne, fans out all of that sweeping freedom and sails in low flight down to the dancers. Its companion leaps and takes off just as quickly.

The dancing cranes stop instantly on hearing the shriek. All of them take to the air. The sky is a dark seething of crane wings. Soon the whole flock is high in the sky, heading towards another familiar place, another marsh. Until their own has been cleansed.

FOR A WHILE we were moving towards each other in some strange channel.

The blood from the gash in my face trickles down on to my jacket. The blood in my veins prickles and tingles like ants in my numbed body. Unsteadily I lean over a puddle to wash. Elsewhere a particle of shame is smarting because of my behavior towards those shy creatures.

Spring in Winter

THE AIR WAS FULL of wet snowflakes, but that didn't matter. Everything was just as it should be; it was a beautiful evening.

A cluster of houses stood there, not large enough to be called a town. The houses had been laid out one by one, without any overall plan, and for this reason there were many unexpected alleys and corners.

Over this a snowstorm was sweeping. At the narrow corners of the mild snowfall met the strong light from the outdoor lamps, and seemed to turn it whiter than white.

And the whiteness poured down into the corners incessantly. The snow near the lamps was trackless. People were indoors.

BUT NOT ALL OF THEM. Out of doors someone was happy on account of the beautiful evening. A short girl was standing close to the wall in the shadow. Or half-shadow, for the mingled snow and lamplight were so strong that the shadows were weakened.

The girl must have been standing there for quite a while; her footprints had been wiped out. She might have tumbled straight out of the night sky.

The girl stood motionless. You could almost believe she was here simply to be snowed under in this lonely place – but she must have had other reasons for coming to stand here glittering.

Snowed under? No, I can't get snowed under, she thought with a bubble of joy. That dark, hard man of iron over there on his block of stone – he can be snowed under, he probably will be snowed under. I can only get warmer and warmer.

The snow won't settle on me, she thought, but if it does, that's all right.

In the meantime the wet flakes fell thickly and heavily onto her shoulders and onto the boyish cap she was wearing on the back of her head, and wherever it found the slightest basis for piling itself up. She already had small drifts of it on her here and there.

Of course the snow is settling on me, she thought when she noticed this. Why shouldn't it? I mustn't move, she thought. I want it like this. Not to be snowed under, but I'll look different, and that's what I want. Everything's different this evening.

He shall see me like this, different, when he comes to meet me.

She stood as motionless as the dark man of iron. He was lonely and deserted. The girl was bubbling inside with joy.

I'll stand like this till he comes. She thought: He's no man of iron; he's a live boy. "Is it you?" he'll say. "Or is all this just snow?" he'll say.

Warmer and warmer.

What does the snow matter then?

IT WAS THE FIRST TIME they were going to meet like this, by agreement. It felt important. It was more important than the evening and the snow.

She thought: What shall I find out?

What is he like? I don't know much about him. I've only seen him a couple of times.

There was music in her and she said:

But I know enough. I've seen enough.

It could snow as much as it liked; she was thinking about the coming meeting.

What will he do?

She was really thinking only this one thing. What will he do?

He'll say "Good evening" and take my hand.

Yes, yes, but what will he do?

He could do many things.

Will his hands come close after a while perhaps? They do that, I know. Someone has done that already, but I'm not going to think about it, because it wasn't as it ought to have been.

Tonight it will be right.

I wonder how much *will* be right this evening?

This was a dangerous train of thought. She completely

forgot her plan about the snow that was going to transform her and make her beautiful. Her thoughts were suddenly as wild as the snowstorm and just as difficult to check. She did not check them until she had taken the measure of all she knew, and it proved to be more than she had expected.

She looked about her and thought: Good thing no one can see what you're thinking.

She shut it away.

Meanwhile it went on snowing, building her up into towers and spires. She carried it well. She was short and lightly built, and seventeen.

HE'S NO OLDER EITHER, she thought. It won't be long now before I shall find out something, whatever it may be. It's almost time. I *wanted* to be first and stand waiting for a long time.

There he is!

Through the whirling snow she caught sight of something coming towards her, seeing it only as something black.

It is, and here I am with all this snow on me!

It was a man or a boy, and he was approaching quickly. But she started in surprise: it was not the boy she was waiting for. It was someone else, from her own neighborhood. Someone she knew slightly. The boy she was waiting for didn't even live here. What does this mean? That he's passing purely by chance, of course. Don't move a muscle because of him.

But he stopped right in front of her and gazed at her as she stood in her heavy robes, her eyes glittering deep in the snow.

"What on earth…?" he began, but did not finish it. Sudden astonishment. He stood there and simply looked at her. She couldn't help it, she looked back at him with that charm she was capable of putting into it; it happened automatically before she had time to feel ashamed. Her eyes were dancing inside the wet snow. It was true that the shadow was not real shadow, after all.

He came close. Suddenly she felt afraid and whispered, "What is it?"

He put out his hand as if to touch the snow piled on her, but withdrew the hand again. It seemed an unconscious gesture.

She whispered, "What is it?"

No answer. He looked at her, thunderstruck. Walked round her, his eyes fixed on her all the time. She did not revolve with him, but whispered into the air after him, "What is it?"

Now he seemed to remember. He gazed into her face. But still he gave no answer to her question. She had stopped glittering at him, even though it was tempting to make use of what she possessed so plentifully.

Suddenly he began talking, fumbling for words.

"Yes, there is something – you mustn't be frightened, you see."

She felt a shaft of ice pass through her. The certainty of what this meant, this thing he had not said, came to her by some mysterious path.

"Isn't he coming?"

He simply looked at her.

She questioned him harshly the second time, and about worse things, knowing it already.

"Has he gone?"

The boy scarcely nodded. This one was a young boy too. His eyes were bewitched now. He simply nodded.

She did not start trembling so that the snow fell off her. She just stood. It was because of his eyes. But she felt as if the snow slid off like an avalanche. There seemed to be a roaring as when an avalanche falls. A cold wind blowing. No, she noticed then that not a flake had fallen off.

"Did he get you to come here and tell me this?"

He would not discuss it. Had probably said enough by nodding. Stand steady, said a voice inside her.

The messenger said something quite different.

"Don't move. You have no idea what you look like."

He didn't manage to say what he wanted. He had taken on himself too powerful a message.

But she knew in her innermost being what she looked

like. He could think what he liked. Nor was she in complete control of herself: sudden tears welled up in her eyes, quickly and briefly. Then it was as if the weather turned milder, and no more came. The young man stood watching.

"That's good," he said when her tears stopped just as suddenly as they had come.

She did not understand. She only asked, "Did he say why?"

He did not answer her. Instead he said something that made her start in surprise.

"I'll unpack you."

Again she heard her thoughts. Without waiting for her permission he did as he wished. He took off the worn pair of gloves he was wearing, and used his bare hands to lift off the snow crown that had built up on the boyish cap.

"Won't be fun any more now," he said. "Think it's stopped snowing."

Yes, it had stopped. She had not noticed before. It was silent and the air was mild. He shook her cap free of snow and put it on again. She was the short girl once more. He unpacked her out of the snow piled on her shoulders. She was confused by his manner of doing all this.

"Unpack you," he said. Over and over again. Fistful by fistful. He took his time.

He unpacked her out of the little snowdrift on her breast. She saw that his fingers were uncertain. And so cold, she thought.

What will he do?

She held her breath, but all he did was go on unpacking her. Bit by bit she turned into an ordinary girl.

"That's that," he said, and had finished at last. But he did not go.

What will he do now?

Again she held her breath. She saw he was trying to say something. He was so strange to look at in everything he did that evening. He said unexpectedly, "You cried."

She had no answer to make. No use denying it.

"I said you cried."

"Maybe I had reason to."

He said, "Maybe. I don't know."

She snapped, "No, you certainly don't know everything!"

"*I'm* not sorry about it," he said, ignoring the interruption. "But that's another matter," he added.

"Why are you standing like that?" she asked.

"Can't I look at you? I feel as if I've never seen you before. It's so strange," he added. He sounded quite helpless.

She replied, "Yes, I suppose it is."

Then he said something: "My fingers are cold from unpacking you out of the snowdrifts all this time."

Something in her responded. "Are they?"

There was nothing more to be said. Both of them knew it. So he said it.

"Maybe I should warm you."

"No," she said quickly.

"All right," he said.

All she said was, "That's good."

He stood looking at her. Everything seemed to be standing on its head. And it was so incredibly mild.

"The snow's quite wet," she said confused.

"Oh yes," he answered, almost as an aside.

But would he go now? She had been a little abrupt with him. So he would probably go.

She stammered, "Are you going?"

He muttered something and there was an embarrassed silence. He mustn't go. She stammered again, "What about those cold fingers of yours?"

He brightened a little and asked, "What about them?"

"Nothing."

"If they really are so cold," she said again.

"Oh no. They're not so cold really. They've been colder."

"Yes, I expect they have."

Everything was standing on its head.

"Why don't you feel them?" he asked.

It was incredibly mild. She let the hands come. The hands, cold as ice, held her close. They made her burning hot. Neither of them could feel cold now.

He said softly: "Awfully good to hold in your hands."

"Yes," she replied, in scarcely a whisper.

Daybreak with Shining Horses

WE MET UNEXPECTEDLY at daybreak one morning. Two young men. The other was called Per. We were acquainted, but not close friends. Now we met on the grass one warm, fine summer morning, before anyone else was up.

Was there something different about Per? As soon as I saw his face, I thought: What is it?

I saw he thought: What is it? when he saw me.

Then one of us said aloud: "What is it!"

It was Per who said it. As if it had nothing to do with him. Perhaps that's how it was. Perhaps my impression of him was distorted.

In any case I could not answer his question. But why was he out of bed at such an unusual time if nothing was the matter?

Neither of us asked again.

FOR MY PART I had got up for reasons that I cannot explain. I had simply done so – as one does when desperately waiting for something.

We looked about us. A warm summer morning. Early, early! was the feeling inside us; it's the only way to describe it. We knew in advance that something was going to happen; it came to us in the moment we met and thought we looked alike. Then we felt this early, early! that there was no other name for.

The landscape had just taken on its distinct solid day-shape with everything in its place – it wasn't because of *that*.

EVERYTHING AS IT SHOULD BE – but was it? We didn't have to look about us to answer no. It was earlier than early inside us. We were wide open. The one looked at the other and realized that our ordinary everyday life had vanished for the time being. If this had been true of only one of us at first, now it was true of both. It had leaped across like lightning.

Suddenly there was a strange shimmer in the air.

I wished he would say: I can see it on you.

He looked at me and said, beyond all reason: "I can see it on you."

I felt myself burn. Don't say any more, I wished, and he didn't.

What was to come of this?

Something is approaching.

Per was no longer his usual self. What had we done to each other?

Without saying anything more, we knew: it is today.

AND IT HAPPENED.

In the first place it came facing the sun, which was odd.

A shining aura settled above the hill, facing the sun, before the sun rose in the opposite direction. We were out as early as that. Whatever else we might have wanted to look at, our eyes turned towards this.

We could not help but believe that what was approaching had its own sources of power. We had a premonition, too, of incredibly long distances to travel across unknown tracts, and of terrific speed – and first and foremost of fascinating things.

Our bodies were buoyant. At the same time we were nudged by a kind of absurd anxiety: the kind that prepares the way for a sudden involvement and happiness. Meanwhile the light approached in a way that we did not understand.

We thought of it as air, but knew it was the glow from

something approaching, just as the sun with its light was approaching over a hill to greet us. Our senses alert, we watched it coming from the opposite direction. We compared it fleetingly and haphazardly to many things. We did not compare the enchantment to anything; it was simply enchantment.

AND INDEED THE ENCHANTMENT sprang up around us in our own landscape as never before, in unexpected forms. In our happy bewitchment we suddenly saw a naked girl at the top of a rock on the other side of the sound. Our own familiar narrow sound. Quite incredibly she stood there waiting, erect, and immovable like ourselves. Like ourselves she was turned towards what was coming, and we understood her so well: understood why she had stripped to face this. We did not know who she was, we did not know where she came from.

When we saw the girl thus confident
as if sprung out of our own thoughts,

on the bank of our own narrow sound,
everything seemed to us to be gentler
within us and without.
We could not yet come closer to it.
We could only stand there.
We said nothing about it to each other,
but saw that the other saw,
so it was no fantasy.
She had stripped to face the same event as us.

IN SILENCE also we saw the gleam grow stronger up on the uneven hillside we were watching.

Perhaps the trees and tussocks of heather up there would soon catch fire? Surely they would not be able to withstand the flames?

But it was not like that either. At the same moment we saw that they did not begin to burn before the still hidden storm of light – we were expecting too much all at once in our excitement.

We were expecting fire, but something else too that would

abruptly and decisively clarify the clouded future, tell us the truth from this day onwards, one early summer morning.

Everything we had wished for, somehow.

More than wished for.

Had wildly wished for.

We included the girl over there across the sound. She was standing as before, waiting as silently as us.

SO IT HAD BEEN worthwhile wishing so wildly.

Was it not our innermost wish we now saw gleaming in the air?

Were we seeing it on its way at last, at the moment when it would soon break over the threshold within us, when it could no longer be stopped by doubt.

The incredible is approaching from over there. It will not leap past us, we shall not be left in our dark vale to watch it go.

What form it had was not our concern. Whether the bush burned or not – not our concern. Our concern was a blazing field of light. Our wish was for explanation. Our concern was what we did not know. We had form on the other side of the sound. We saw it with our boys' eyes, proud that such should exist on our own home ground. We included *that* in the shared mood of exhilaration we were in. Our naked girl would enter the approaching field of light as an assured point of rest, as a kind of quivering anchorage in what we, in spite of everything, possessed.

We did not know her, as she stood there sparkling, but she was one of us. We almost felt that it was we who had come to meet her.

WE STIFFENED: there it was up on the hill, shining among the trees and bushes.

First only as light.

Nothing caught fire there, but the sight of it was so strong that it blinded us.

We did not see whether it was the light of truth; there were horses, horses, a wave of shining horses, or a waterfall of them.

A waterfall of horses over the crest, pouring down our hillside like an unpent dam. But without noise, soundless as the shadows and the light. This light would fill us, we would become capable of doing something remarkable, we suddenly persuaded ourselves.

HUSH, we thought as the searing notion presented itself – that we were in reality seeing nothing, but that instead we were about to die. Thus it could shift and become distorted in the space of a moment.

Why is nobody riding on the horses? Why is there no thundering of numberless hooves?

It is death. Nobody could ride a horse made of light, surely?

I am dying.

And in the same instant, like a stab: Already? No, no.

Hush, we said to the thought, but it would not obey, it went on nagging us, spoiling our great joy, trying to destroy our exhilaration and the happy impulses we were beginning to feel. Then I saw that Per was pointing like a rescuer across the sound, pointing at the girl who was standing on the rock as before, waiting as before. Everything was changed again, we were not about to die, we were alive and more than alive, we were open and ready to be filled with what was coming.

IT POURED ON DOWN the hillside. An unbridled dance of shining horses.

And on that hillside.

Ours, our hillside. There these inflaming visions were to be played out.

The hillside – where the dew had many a time collected on my shoulders through the night, in the grass beneath trees dense with leaf, where the darkness had been fearful and enticing. The arm of the brook beside which I had sat thinking illicit, strange thoughts. And the place where the cliffs hid in the tall grasses edging them, turning the drops into terrifying pitfalls. On this hillside, where I had sat thinking until it seemed as if I had never really been there at all, the rushing wave of light swept down as runaway horses. Our wild exhilaration was sweeping along, making straight for us.

To change us in some way?

Irregular gleams flickered between the trees.

Tall grasses and stiff angelica heads slapped against the horses' dancing flanks, their gleaming flanks, it was quite beyond reason and there was no thunder of hooves, they were noiseless. Since there was no sound, our tongues were paralyzed. No one could shout in that silence. No one dared to look across the sound now; we were standing stiffly to receive them.

Thinking that now everything was different.

We were not to die, but to be created anew, on our familiar hillside.

BEFORE LONG it looked as if the whole hillside were alight – as if our wish had come true. How could we tell? We stood there in a kind of elation. Tensely we saw that the terrifying cliffs did not exist: the stampede swept straight over them and nothing happened, none of them disappeared in the pitfalls, the web of light was unbroken.

And then:

They are here.
What will happen?
Welter of thoughts
forwards, backwards,
the moment the stampede began,
reached us,
bore us up and shattered us.
It cannot be spoken, but
straight towards us,
straight, straight, our desire.
We saw no eyes,
we saw spears of light;
not those either, we
were in the centre,
lifted like down and like silk,
at the same time it was scorching fire.
It felt like becoming many,
many out of one.
Not like that either:
it sped right through us,

not stopped by our presence in the way,
it rushed right through us
 – and we shone too.
We knew now was the time, but
time for what?
Per, my friend, lay on the ground
bow-shaped, and shone.
He jumped up again, touching me
and at once I shone.
I told him: "You're shining!"
He called out, elated:
"Don't forget!"
No more, made dumb,
dumb by new currents,
what he wished to say lost.
He was here, out of reach.
His severed cry floated
up the fiery hillside, as the cloud shadows do,
the fleeting cloud shadows on an innocent everyday.

Do not forget? What did he mean?
And where was I?
Wild groping in the brain,
and the first already long past.
We stood mingled with new, never seen things,
the nameless ones, and
in the midst of commotion dear things that *have* names:
lovely angelica from my own hillside.
Angelica man-tall at my side rustled
its sunshades as if there was something important
to tell me
which I should fathom.
Fathom, fathom – the generous message
did not reach me
and Per lay on the ground shining,
no, not shining, a field of light.
The last horses were streaming through,
time was up.
Too late to reach them,

too late to hold anything back.
Too late. What had been wrong?
Pointless groping.
The sunshades rustled, but uselessly.
The stampede was already leaving.
We were already behind it,
as if we had never been.
What was it that had not been grasped?
Had no one stretched out their hands?

We saw the shining stampede depart.
Saw without knowing,
as if we had never been.
Watching and watching as it rushed along.
We had not grasped it.
The field of light, Per, again took form
and stood groping with empty hands.
He had not grasped it.
We did not speak.

It all had happened at whirlwind speed,
passing through us and passing on.
We still could see the stampede of light
sweeping over the sound without a flicker
of the surface. Trembling we watched.
Sweeping over the water, turning the sound into fire.
On the other side our naked girl
dissolved into a thousand winking stars.

That too.
We saw that, then?
But without understanding.
It happened before our very eyes:
dissolved into a thousand winking stars.
It rushed on. *Had she grasped it?*
We saw without understanding: had she
grasped it?
Saw, unable to think.

A thousand winking stars, we thought, like
some holy shock.

Death had not come, we stood as before on the
sweet slope.
We had not grasped the greatness
while it was here.
We did not speak.

A flower of angelica, man-tall at my side
rustled with all its sunshades,
rustled in our own silent storm. Already
the field of light was beyond another crest.
No figure stood on the rock across the sound.

The Drifter and the Mirrors

LEANING OUT over the water and the mirrors.

They twinkle and bewitch.

Be drawn towards the slime? Don't think. Don't think. Climb away from the slime? Don't think. The slime was imagination? Don't think. Nobody knows what flatters and bewitches.

BEWILDERMENT increases in the presence of the mirrors. Leaning over as far as possible, to the point where one almost topples in. The deep water reaches right up to the rock here; tilt too far, and it would all be over. But there is still a foothold left in the heather and the scents and the hopelessness, and in all that hounds one on and that one wishes to be rid of.

Leaning over, thinking, or at any rate trying to think. No use. No thoughts there.

Leaning over, knowing one is about to slip. The thought of slipping becomes stronger the longer one looks down into the water. The picture down there is distinct; one can read it like a book. There is no current to pull the features awry; the mirror does not deform anything. There is a current deep down; one thinks of that.

Yet the face is deformed now, distorted and unlike itself, the result of the misfortunes that have come like avalanches – there behind him, where he has left his half-lived life. What has really happened? He meets his own shocked eyes down below.

Leaning a little bit more.

Meeting an eye that says: Come.

It's as bad as that. It does not matter what the eye is now that everything has gone so perversely and painfully aground.

Bewilderment has set in. Soon the picture will begin to glide. Begin to pull and bind and distort him. His own eyes are there no longer; he sees a fragmented eye and it numbs the link with his mind.

A stranger on one's own shore, become chillingly lonely. He did not consider the strength of his own resistance while there was still time. While there was still resistance.

At the pace where he has come from yawn two great sorrows and a couple of shattering defeats. Never back there, he says in this twisted moment. No, your last card has been played, he reads in the sinister eye in the water.

There can be nothing more.

Something must be done. Done. Halted by the water, and the pull from deep down, that's what he thinks – because he has the inverted mirrors facing him.

Slipping a little more.

THE MIRRORS in the bewildered eyes down below have come alive and work on him with all their might. They suck him to them. He understands better and better that this is where he is to go. Now. The picture dissolves, then rearranges itself. There is no way past the water-mirrors. They increase in strength and fascination as they throw inverted images up from the depths. He is ensnared by them, and believes blindly in what they tell him.

Leaning over more. Still he does not slide down. Staring at the picture which is supposed to be himself. Soon he has forgotten that he is looking at his own reflection. Nor could he have recognized any part of it. The eye is no longer a human eye. It is transformed; it calls and says come, and the mirrors charm capriciously between. They have such drawing power because this is happening on the outermost edge of the abyss.

Tossing forwards and backwards the whole time. The brief time; this will not last long.

Yet – the flashing of the mirrors that do not exist, with colours in polished mirror edges that promise better things. The exhausted man on the rock has no real resistance to offer. The outcome must be decided already.

They lure him on. Come.

Not quite ready. His feet still seem to be caught in what he has trampled on.

Come now.

He cannot distinguish one thing from another, what is down or what is up. The mirrors have done this to him. But he does not let himself slide yet. Come down, he hears, kindly and insistently. He leans over lower and farther.

Come, he hears, and he could not possibly hear anything more beautiful.

The features down below are about to lose their normal

shape, worn away by the hard struggle. Only the eyes and what is saying Come. In all the confusion something is repeating, as evenly as a clock: Come. There is a tempo in it that is a part of the attack on him.

He does not know that it is his own power of allurement and seduction that is facing him from the head in the water. He watches it like a stranger, or a distant, kind friend.

The most beautiful word in existence approaches him from two directions. It is double, and the distance between up and down is continually shortening. In reality the gap gets deeper, in reality it is sinking a little all the time; something important is being snuffed out.

But what is important and not important when one's own features have disintegrated? The tired man on the brink of the river can find no reasonable explanation for this.

The most beautiful word in existence joins itself from above and below, and then everything is ready for action. He does not see the sharp boundary he is crossing. His feet begin to slide out of their foothold without a signal from any central place.

He is not even aware that it is he who is falling at this moment. Because it feels just as much up as down.

But he is setting out on his journey down. Hold after hold up here must release him. He slides down as quietly as a shadow can glide into deep water. There was no height; he was just above the surface. No ripples result. A little agitation in the mirror, that is all. It happens gently, and at first up and down do not change places.

He has let go of the last hold.

His thoughts are twisted into a hopeless tangle. He lets himself slide down in shock because his face broke up as he was watching. It had become natural to slide into it. He had already become the other, the one who was calling.

He scarcely notices the transition. A little jerk of cold from somewhere. The eye that compelled this journey is not with him, nor the thoughts about what led him here. Now explosions of newness are crashing over him.

HIS MIRROR WAS SMASHED and vanished, but only in the instant when the eye struck against its own averted surface. As he sinks he manages to open his eyes again, confused beneath the surface of the water, and sees mirrors or mirror images in improbable patterns. They reflect and flash with improbable objects, while he moves downwards and the shortage of air begins to throttle him. Very soon this becomes urgently painful. He starts to flail his arms and struggle wildly for air, without thinking or remembering where the air is, frightened and flailing his arms more and more.

Everything at once. Things happen that make no impression on him. They stream through him in an instant. He manages to grasp a little of it.

It grows light around him. He has brought some shining pearls with him into the deep water. Nothing strange in that: the mirrors are standing up there at all angles. The pearls shine about his head and shoot small dots of light down through his path. He strikes them with his flailing arms and there are many more.

Suddenly they are no longer with him. It grows darker, but not completely dark.

Everything at once. Threads that go out from him and into the denser darkness a short distance away. Curious glimpses from the mirrors' edges and from his own eye-miracle and the pearls that he still thinks he is flailing. Objects do not stay still, they are carried away; everything is carried away down here by a current, slowly, with a gentle consideration that dwells in its enormous strength. The man also is seized by it and is carried gently and surely away. Away and at the same time upwards through the layers of water, towards the surface.

He has no thoughts about it.

For him everything is happening at once. He is straining for air. Thunder is surrounding in his ears. His clothes hang heavily on him, yet he is rising.

Meanwhile he becomes numb and semi-conscious. Pearls and glimpses of mirrors and everything shining around him are snuffed out. And nothing is calling. Gradually relaxing he is carried at an angle up and up – because of his lighter weight and the laws controlling the currents in the deep water.

Nor does he miss in his semi-conscious state the dance of the mirrors that happened so suddenly. It has been left behind somewhere, he has forgotten about it. And no one is calling.

No, no one is calling down here. It was imagination, and far distant from the darker matters that are forcing themselves in on him now: whether he is to be snuffed out too. It has almost reached that point, but he is still moving at an angle up to where the air is. He does not know it; he knows nothing now. He dimly perceives a shadow passing by, with a burning spot in it. It seems larger than it ought to be, because it came from somewhere in the middle of a streak of flame. From the surface he knows nothing about. Then there is nothing. But the surface is not far away now. The breaking point comes nearer all the time. Increasingly heavy, choking, he knows no more about that than about the rest.

Knows little now.

Darker below.

Is there something?

What is something?

Nobody here.

Twilight below. More and more twilight.

Thunder in my ears.

He has no notion of the current down here. The current has abruptly changed direction: something turns him, and all of a sudden he sinks straight down.

It doesn't matter; he notices nothing.

Then the man is standing in the slime once more. It is not quite dark; the water is shallower, so that a little daylight penetrates down to the muddy river bed. There is a shimmer here, but the half-snuffed out man does not know about it.

His feet are planted in the slime, weighted by all the earthly loads he has dressed himself in. Thunder is echoing in his ears. The iron grip on his throat and chest is loosening. If he sees anything, it is his own fantasy. It all happens so fast.

But life is obstinate; it will not allow this to happen.

HE SENSES THAT OBJECTS are passing him. It is all fantasy. Strange shadows go past. Forests go past. Oceans of people go past. Then an unexpected streak of light moves from another direction and clarifies matters a little: he feels

that he is *standing on something*. He jerks into consciousness from his half-bursting condition. His heavy boots are
standing on earth. His brain clears, he kicks wildly in order
to get rid of the boots, to get lighter. He has an inkling
about making himself lighter and floating upwards. Here
is a chance to go upwards. He is desperate for air but bends
down and manages to get off the boots. He flails his arms
and gets his jacket off too. He is half dead, but savage. And
now he is lighter, now he is in the current once more.

He thinks he is shouting at the top of his voice while
doing this. He thinks he is struggling with monstrous beasts.
Kicked up slime whirls round him and is drawn away; he is
lighter and rises upwards into yet another kind of current.
He does not feel this; everything is again at a distance. But
it has all happened with incredible speed since he let himself
slide down. He is still alive.

He is greeted by a glimmer that keeps a hold on his life
during the final turns of the reel, as a few wild pictures
unfold. He does not see it visually, only feeling it as a nudge.

He will soon be up.

Then it becomes huge and different. He gets part of his face up to the surface – and now air and water seem to leap in fragments. He does not know what it is, but something from inside himself leaps into the air. Great mountains fall away from him, he shoots up to the sky. He inhales all the air in the world. He knows no more than that.

He is not aware that he is floating on the surface now. His face guides itself so that it can get at the air. The water laps over it now and then, but he is able to lift himself up slightly and draw in air as if with his last few breaths.

The gentle, superior force of the river seizes him at once and carries him slowly along. As yet he is scarcely aware of it.

ONCE AGAIN THE MIRRORS are playing with him. They are active in the sunshine. For there is sunshine and daylight up here. He has been in an artificial night. Sometimes he bobs beneath the surface, but comes up again each time and manages to breathe as much as is necessary. He is exposed to all the rays he can scarcely bear, all kinds of shadows, all kinds of half-sleeping fantasies.

He has come to a part of the river where occasional logs of timber are floating downstream. No lumberjacks are in sight. A log bumps into his side and, without knowing what he is doing, he throws his arms round it in a convulsive grip that he never loosens. It holds him up and keeps his face above water. Together they float downstream. He does not think about it. He is scarcely aware of it.

No people and no buildings on the banks of the river. When he left in his despair he had walked far into the woods, where the broad waterway flows alone, and only then did he approach the water.

There are woods here; otherwise it is quite deserted. There is nobody on the shore to see that something unusual is floating out there.

That's not quite correct. Something sees it. Birds in the air see it, have already seen it. They behave in several ways. Some keep silent, others set up a cry in whatever way they can. A couple of crows are accompanying him from tree to tree, keeping silent, following, biding their time.

The drifter himself on the water, can he hear anything?

Can he see? He does not yet understand what there is to see and hear. Nothing is clear to him. Bird calls and gleams of sunshine alternate with ploughing under water – and thus it continues. He is blind to the succession of pictures. He half sleeps his way forward, drawing in fresh, life-giving air and coughing out water. He drifts imperceptibly and continually southward, past deserted banks, clinging to the log. The water-mirrors throb with distorted sunshine and all that is dangerously and confusing to someone like him.

Suddenly he shrieks. Something has snapped at his foot down there. It released him at once, but the resulting smart that he imagines streams through his body as the water is streaming outside it. It wakes him up.

He kicks out blindly. After this struggle panic mounts up easily in the chaotic and depleted space inside him. Then he feels a fresh bite or sting. Down in the depths.

He is going to be devoured by something, he believes in his delirium. A lightning flash from a mirror told him of it. Perhaps he is half devoured already? What can he know about it? The mirrors, and his own position close to death, can tell him what no other can.

He starts to say something that was meant to be, "No, no!" A bellowing.

The call was loud. It rolls to the shore. The two crows who are following and waiting flutter out from the nearest tree and take a long sweep before returning to hide in another tree close by.

The call comes back as an echo, and spreads in the vast silence. It tears a veil in front of him – and the mirrors strike with all the incitement at their command. In cracks and openings, which the harsh treatment has opened and closed again, there they attack.

Come, they say. Just like the last time, on land.

He does not understand it.

Come? What does that mean?

No, something in him answers, purely by accident.

He is indifferent really.

All the same it is a moment of awakening. He is close beside rustling shores. The quiet is rustling in the treetops. The briefest of awakenings. He is still holding on to a log.

The quiet also brings scents with it from land to the half dead man who is floating past like any piece of driftwood. The strange smell that has accompanied him from the slime mingles with them. Birds are flying above him, following the same course as himself, and the water, and the mirrors. In a flash it appears to him as a great, rustling journey.

It does not occur to him that these are birds of prey following him; he likes them. Everything is out on a journey. And now he can take a nap and rest for a while, he thinks vaguely, and is on the point of plunging down into desperation again.

He is hindered by a small promontory jutting out fairly close to him. It suggests the idea of making a crawling motion with his arms in order to try to swim ashore. Nothing comes of it; he has no extra strength at all. Presumably he will have to be satisfied with floating passively on a river.

But it looks as if he will not get any sleep. At that instant he knocks his skull on something with a thud that is repeated many times. It is a sinking log with only the root sticking up above water. The man has his own log to cling to, but opens his eyes wider all the same, *sensing* that he has a means of saving himself for the time being.

They float past the sinking log, which resembles a dark, empty face sticking up.

It is a blessed relief to come to full knowledge of the log, to hold on to something that does not go under at once. But something is fluttering close above him. The bird and death. The bird alights on the log and inspects it closely, but flies up again. No death yet, apparently. The grey-black bird flaps its wings heavily and in annoyance as it flies out of sight in order to wait a little longer.

It looks as if he will be in the company of the bird at the last. No savage death after all: a supine, quiet death, the kind that dwells in the hollows in the woods and which the crows never miss. The man understands something, and is about to lose his hold on the log, but quickly seizes it again when the bird rises. Wood is a capital material to hold on to in deep water. Not down there, he thinks.

THE ANNOYING, MEDDLESOME mirrors are stubbornly trained on the drifter. There they are, wherever he turns his exhausted head, adding still more confusion to all that he wants to think about. Can all this really be true?

It is not true, he tries to say as soon as it clears for a moment. I don't see them. Nothing has been true today, he thinks.

Up and down. In a little while he is not up to holding on to the log any more; he lets go. At once he bobs under, long enough to notice how various creatures down there shoot away from him sideways, creatures that have collected and followed him on his journey. He catches small side glances from them and gathers that they are not friendly. But they are too small to swallow him whole.

He is below for only an instant, then grasps the log above him and floats up again. He has no energy, except the small amount needed to cling to the saving yellow timber. He is not thinking deeply about weight and sinking, but he senses that he is lighter.

Very well, rise up to the open surface again. A thought

forms through all obstacles, the thought that this is extraordinary. Something more too, but he stops and comes no further.

The beginning of something: that this is extraordinary.

A short while after: How much is needed?

He comes no further.

This was thought in the fresh air, for his head is on the surface again. Up on the shining expanse, in the gentle pull of the waterway.

He still does nothing himself, merely holds on, as still as a mouse, floating along and thinking the thought that it is extraordinary. It has stayed with him like a solace together with the log he lost and found again.

The current has hold of him, and the current seems kindly disposed and will perhaps set him carefully on land sooner or later like any other piece of driftwood. Like any other reject. They usually end up on land.

Don't come here! he thinks all of a sudden. A new shudder of thought had opened.

I'm thinking about the bird, he thinks.

Don't come.

Come, say the water-mirrors in their own way, from their own point of view.

He drifts with the current towards all that must be ahead, without bothering about it in the slightest. With him he has his retinue of birds and death and the water that he will never be rid of, and the fantasy mirrors.

Come! insist all the others. He will not.

HE THINKS: What is this? Over and over again. What does this mean? Where am I journeying?

He does not think, Is this for me?

Sleep. Dead tired.

Can't sleep. No one may sleep. There is a bird in the air waiting for those who sleep.

Sailing through fire and water. It may look like water but it is full of fire. Sailing through aeons of time away from a threatening fire. Sailing in a great retinue, which is the water, along the banks, across the sky. Together with the bird who keeps company with death. Together with the countless trees on land.

The mirrors are there too, and fill him with many fragments of turmoil, bringing back memories and covering them up again before they are distinct.

He is reminded of a number of the scents on land. They do not reach him. The mirrors nag at it and he goes along with them. Solid land. Earth, trees, grass. And aeons of time. He gains a hint, too, of all the rest, which does not exist when your head is only just rippling the surface.

And a wall of faces that has appeared, it seems to him. Impossible to be rid of. The bewildered wall of faces lined up along the shores, so close that they can only be seen as a wall. The mirrors display them in their merciless fashion. The wall and the pleasant land. He sails past. The wall shuts off the scents.

The mouths in the wall. He will not think about it. He sails past with aversion.

They are calling something.

I won't.

The mirrors sway, enjoying themselves.

There are faces that crack and are not yawns, are not faces, except to resemble the face of a flower that one can hide under. But one cannot do that when sailing past. One sees them – they leap out and are simply there.

Through aeons of time.

He sees faces in the wall shrink and disintegrate like ashes, and at the same moment there stands another severe, staring person in the empty space. It is all familiar, he has had it all around him, in love and in aversion; the mirrors have found it, the mirrors have aeons of time.

The mouths are calling about something, out across the water and far beyond the drifter. He cannot hear what it is.

The black birds sweep above him in silent patience. They fly on ahead and wait further down. They follow, after waiting behind. The drifter goes too slowly for them. But their patience has been won through aeons of time and has always received its just reward.

THE DRIFTER SAILS with his motley retinue through the landscape. It is his own countryside and at the same time one that is completely unknown to him. They are his shore and his birds, his face in the wall, his cry in the call.

His own riddles wall him in, as he himself was a riddle on the paths on land.

His own sorrow is there too. Sorrow that neither he nor anyone else can explain.

GRADUALLY the knowledge of what it is he is journeying away from awakens in him. The mirrors search along the shores and find it whether it is there or not. Sometimes the journey takes him close to the banks and in other places farther out, but the mirrors find it. They have many shapes and many errands. They flash and force their way through, reaching their goal in spite of obstacles and layers of slime. They cut right through it all. They may not cease to be a part of him.

Things may be dancing on the banks, but theirs is no dance of joy. The drifter cannot grasp it, since only a part of him is alive, seeing to it that his nose is kept out of the warm summer water instead of letting the water snuff him out, as it would prefer to do.

Now the known is unknown. Those he knows are not with him today, he pretends. He says nothing about having fled from them.

Nor does the drifter realize that he is moving so slowly, that only the precious time is passing. He mutters about aeons of time like a simpleton.

I was my cry, he thinks with incredulity. He is not uttering any cries, yet it is I who am crying, he tells himself.

He examines the mouths in the wall as he says so – and of course it is his cry. He can draw breath, he is not dying.

He seems to have no body, he cannot yet use his arms in order to swim. But he has with him the large retinue on the earth, in the air and in the water, and senses it along with the wind and shadows and muted cries that are found on the long waterways.

There are more and more of them. They come because of the pull of the journey. They are released from their old ways and join in before they are aware of it. It is a mighty pull, and offers no comfort, digging them up, prying them loose and forcing them into it.

Creatures large and small, but not a single human being.

The innocent drifter in the lead has gradually become a mere pretext.

A NEW ELEMENT.

The living bark of a dog explodes from behind the trees on the shore. Loud and giving warning, with the correct silence afterwards. Then a whole series of signals from the hidden dog.

A house? Not a house to be seen. That is his first thought. It was a shocking sound. There is nobody in sight. The watchdog keeps himself hidden.

The dog's bark is echoed back from the hillside opposite. This must encourage him, for he goes on barking. Sounds arc hurled past each other and split in two – meaningless, but unspeakably joyous among all that is here already.

The man in the water lets it rain down over him. He is

lying in the middle of the din and feels curves and stripes forming in his skull during the ten-fold howling of the dog. None of his own cries have been heard. *This* is the cry. A growl starts up in his throat, in the slime and the taste of the water, and he startles himself when he opens his mouth wide and howls more horribly than he realizes: "Wowwow wow!"

There is a sudden silence on the shore. Then a frightened bark. What the man said must have sounded dreadful to the dog's ears; he only manages to squirt a sound out from between his teeth.

The current gives the drifter a little nudge. The way south is open.

The drifter is inflamed by all his bewildering visions.

What is this? The first contact after having been at the bottom in the slime.

"Wow wow!" he hollers. A language he has only just learnt.

The hills reply.

Then the dog goes wild, with terror, joy or insult. He forgets to stay hidden, leaps out on to an isolated rock on the shore and barks at the top of his voice, abusing the object he can see out there.

The man with his nose above water lifts himself up as far as he can and frees his mouth. They greet each other in angry or possibly unpleasant terms, filling the valley with this hostile language.

The drifter has excited himself far too much, beyond his strength. In the middle of a howl he collapses once more, and gets a dunking. He has enough to do paying attention to more immediate matters.

The dog falls silent and disappears.

The journey continues as before. The drifter survives the latest dunking too, but is down in a trough of misery where even the provocative mirrors mean nothing.

What now?

It is evening.

IT IS THE ONSET of evening at the end of this wearying day. A warm fine evening.

The traveller has not gone very far. He has not yet come to any villages. The current allows itself ample time to exert its pressure.

A beautiful evening for those who could appreciate it. A drifter in the current like himself is not among them. He is floating southward as a part of the hopeless tangle, as a damaged consciousness.

But he is in contact with the dog.

After the first skirmish things go more gently. It turns out that the dog is keeping up with him behind the bushes, as the patient crow is keeping up with him still from tree to tree. The crow has not yet lost its faith in a meal.

The dog has other, hidden motives. Contact with man. The howl told of a web of things known to the dog that the drifter in the current took up blindly and can answer.

Perhaps it is this that sustains him through the struggle when he is about to give up. He does not sink; he has the thought of the dog.

At each promontory the dog meets him and gives a short, sharp bark, no longer hostile. It waits for an answer and gets one. 'Woof!' comes the reply from out on the water, muffled or loud, according to his strength. He growls in dog fashion, quite taken up with this unfamiliar language and concentrating on it with all his might.

At every little promontory the dog stands waiting.

The echo that sang out with them has finished. The valley sides have taken on a different shape and do not send sounds back. They are frothing with the ripeness of late summer, but keep silent.

The evening is stealing on. The sun that once was reflected in the mirrors has gone; no one will be bewitched by it now. The twilight is setting in, and will bewitch instead. The dog has fallen silent, like one who has come home and forgotten everything out of doors. The crow disappears and will have to go to bed hungry. Evening is evening. It will probably find him tomorrow.

The drifter feels that much has gone. He appreciated his splendid retinue. He tries out his newly acquired language again and brings out a weak 'woof' a couple of times, without getting any answer. It did not carry far enough.

The lack of an answer upsets him, making him angry and depressed. He lies on his back with his mouth open ready to call should he have the strength, and in any language. The water is so still that it does not splash over his gaping jaws. He does not move a muscle – that time is past. He clings tightly to the log with his arm, his eyes wide open to the cloudy sky. The sky became cloudy just after sunset. The man lies looking at a darkening ceiling without thinking about it. Gaping at it. Nobody sees this. It is the kind of moment that nobody witnesses.

He is still afloat on the strength of the contact with the dog. He moves his lips slightly.

IMMEDIATELY afterwards the back of his head knocks against something hard. He is drifting head first.

Perhaps it hurt a little, but he does not know what pain is any more and it makes no impression on him. But it stops his forward movement. The restless current swings his body slowly towards solid ground. There he lies without coming any further.

Shortly after a large bird shoots over.

The drifter, who is gaping up into the evening sky and appears to be dead, does not even start. He lies still where he has drifted against the shelf of rock.

The bird comes back and drops heavily, alighting on his breast and folding its wings. The drifter starts and notices it. He writhes and shrieks, an ordinary human shriek.

The shriek is piercing. The bird, which is a quiet night bird, rises quickly and noiselessly. It had made a mistake.

The sudden movement fills the drifter's mouth with water. The shock passes like a ray through his paralyzed body. He thrashes about him with the one arm, as if the bird were still there. He strikes his hand against something, and seizes it. It is a tree-root. A tree at the outermost edge of the shore where the water has washed away the soil. He has run aground on stones and roots.

His hands dig into the roots of their own accord. Both hands. He is lying on solid ground and can scrabble like this without thinking. A reminder goes through his brain about holding fast, about pulling. He is able to do it because of the sudden stimulation. He can drag himself a little way out of the everlasting water. His feet are still lying in it, that doesn't matter. There he lies. He is seized with a great fit of trembling.

The twilight deepens, very slowly; he can see objects around him, but is not sure what they are. He can see with his eyes. He moves and says something. He sees the water and trembles. *Water?* he wonders. His thoughts are still paralyzed.

He thinks he sees the bird approaching in the twilight and barks a loud, scared yell of terror at it.

Something answers him.

Promptly an answer comes from some way off, the frightened baying of a dog once more, excited and aggressive baying, as if at something unlawful.

The man hesitates. He cannot produce a sound.

The dog goes on barking.

If he had wanted to answer he could not have got it in, for

the dog is exciting himself more and more. He must be at the other end of the beach now. The drifter lies still, rocking in this rhythmical sound without attempting to join in.

A fresh series of unrelated pictures. It seems as if channels of light are passing through him, regardless of the late evening and the twilight. Curious channels of light. He cannot link them with anything. Impossible to understand when you are dead almost all over.

The dog continues with its warnings. In the drifter they turn into visions that he destroys at once. Then the dog stops. What does this mean?

Another sound from the shore.

"Hoy!" calls someone, even louder than the dog.

"Hoy! Hi!" he calls.

What is happening? Everything comes to a standstill – and then seems to go up in the air. The human call clangs in his ears. His paralyzed thought sequences shiver with tension. His excitement flares up, and he replies like thunder, so it seems to him, as best he can, "Wow wow!"

He cannot find anything to say except the dog's cry. It was

not what he had meant, but what he was able, to say. What he had meant to say had suddenly become far too perplexing and far too much to be shouted.

He paws at it with stiff fingers, with clenched fists in a web delicate as hair. Impossible, it falls to pieces.

He listens, lying on his back. He has drawn his feet up. His hands cling convulsively to the root.

Something is happening over there. No more calling. Something is happening.

He can hear it; something is approaching him. He hears growling and a few quiet barks, and some quiet splashes that awaken a memory. He cannot reach it.

Then he sees it in the semi-darkness. All of a sudden a boat appears. It is approaching from land, it is alongside at once.

The drifter sees it, but he has seen so much this afternoon. He sees this new vision approach, large and strange. He twists towards it.

"Be quiet, will you?" someone in the boat says to someone else.

"Hi there, what's the matter?" comes again from the boat. Someone is standing up in the boat speaking to him.

The drifter finds it impossible to answer. If he were to say anything just now, everything would shatter and sink to the bottom. He is careful not to say woof, either, because it is not suitable. An avalanche of things from another existence is rushing in on him. He is speechless.

The boat is made fast to a root at the water's edge, and a man and a dog on a leash take the few paces towards the drifter. When the dog reaches him he gives a cautious woof.

The drifter answers with a low woof, out of the enormous upheaval he feels is approaching.

The stranger leans over in a friendly fashion and acts as if he had heard nothing.

"I expect you'd rather come home with me, instead of lying here?" he asks, in such a normal fashion that it sounds unnatural.

It means nothing to the drifter. He is busy clarifying matters and does not reply. He is putting his thoughts in order. The mirrors have reached his channels of light, many of them and very close. They are transmitting their pictures through him. It is wonderful. He understands more and more. His body is still powerless.

The stranger grips him strongly under the arms and lifts him. He manages to carry him. His feet drag numbly along the ground. The dog walks close beside them without making a sound.

Beside the boat the man is forced to put his burden down. The wet body is as heavy as stone.

"You're heavy."

No answer.

The man points at the boat. "Boat," he explains, pointing again, his voice tense with concern.

No answer. Putting his thoughts in order.

"Boat," says the man, with emphasis. "Boat on water," he says.

Yes! A glimmer of life then.

In confused mirror glimpses and an awakening sense of order he sees that it is a boat, and knows what boat means.

THAT WAS A GOOD GIFT from the mirrors. With the boat as his starting point he can go further and understand more and more.

He finds his voice. "Boat," he replies, clearly, with understanding. It is too dark to see that his face has lighted up, but perhaps it can be heard.

The man cautiously pulls the heavy drifter close up to the boat. They say no more to each other.

The dog sits as if waiting for something, and the man says to him, "Yes, you'd better have a sniff at him, good dog."

The dog does so for an instant, and then jumps into the boat.

The man pulls the drifter in over the gunwale, afraid he will be unable to bear it.

The Wasted Day Creeps Away on Its Belly

NOBODY TALKS ABOUT the wasted day.

The wasted day creeps away on its belly.

Only the chairs stand upright in place, in the halls, in the halls. Those empty chairs of ours in the halls – because this day is over.

The day that was no day, is over. We nodded and went out, went home. The day turned into a day of shame and will never show itself again. Nothing is nothing, the day is past, it is evening and the wind is rising.

The skulls went home. We sit there no longer. We nodded to everything, giving our approval. A nod is a nod. Then it is evening, and the wind is rising.

The chairs are deserted, nothing was done. Nothing will be done tomorrow either – but we shall occupy the chairs and the nods will be nodded, and the wind – yes, the wind is rising.

NOTHING WAS CHANGED, neither ourselves nor others. The day must creep out of the room with it. In its place the room slowly fills with dusk. Someone is calling from outside, but a call from outside does not reach in to the stricken day. The day that has been destroyed – it began as pale pink veils on the mountain peaks in the morning.

WE KNEW THIS and settled ourselves comfortably in our chairs. We were alert and farsighted.

NOTHING.

How much can be betrayed by a nod?

Nobody used his head to prevent misfortune and misery. The day creeps on its belly out of the room, to find a hiding-place far down in the cellars, where the rats lurk with their long naked tails. We sat in the chairs all the day long and nodded a costly span of time down to the rats. We knew everything.

The day creeps on its belly like a snake, and breaks in pieces in order to make off into thousands of hiding places:

in the wilderness, in the upper reaches of lakes, between the blocks of stone in ancient mountain slides. Never out again – until the merciless clock strikes. The betrayed day, once so splendidly equipped, has no chance now. When the clock strikes it is too late.

Deeper and deeper among the blocks, among stones the size of houses – where it is always dark, and there are always nameless creatures. Among such as these end parts of the wasted day, with small, dark creatures that nibble each other a little in the shell, that bide their time in peace.

OUR CHAIRS are in position, ready for the next time. The wiseacres were there, reclining indolently or sitting nervously and stiff, but all of us sat nodding – and now it is evening and stormy.

The day has hidden itself in everything that can provide shelter. The day bores in beneath the grass on the graves, to the skulls lying there. Wiseacres who probably sat in the chairs once upon a time. They did not prevent misfortune and misery. They are darkened skulls; it is pitch dark around them. The day comes down to them and vanishes, as smoke vanishes, and as the most dangerous secrets vanish.

The grass grows over them and fades, and the snow falls and the nights fall, and the spring matures and fades. A tiny speck sits there on one leg, biding its time, and does not know why it does so.

AND THEN there's the water.

The water laps alongside. Laps against all kinds of shores, all kinds of walls, all kinds of hard rocks.

Water for soothing, for washing, for setting limits. Water for expansion and for obliteration. The ocean for breaking down boundaries. The ocean for destruction, for ruin. The wash of its waves passes through the embankments like weighty signals.

But slow, friendly signals too. Something nobody has yet learnt, but signals. Water is spacious and silent. The lake has enormous depth. The day sinks through layer upon layer of darkening lake, which meet and are silent. Below exists what is nameless, where the disfigured can dissolve.

Lapping in the small lakes in the forest. Signals all the way to the graves, from the lakes in the forest. There are graves and the lapping of lakes around graves, and everything that exists is a single. Shores of peat, water lilies above shifting lake-beds, layer below layer, where what is heavy as lead goes through without hindrance.

THE WIND IS RISING.

The lake will be dangerous.

The wind from the ocean blows on to the land in the darkness.

It is not quite dark, though; there is a moon. The wind sweeps in the night and howls at the chairs from the night-side. The wind grows stronger and blows the doors open, sweeping in towards the empty mass of chairs – but is stopped abruptly as if by a sudden thought. The doors slam shut again. Windows opened by the wind slam shut. It is as if all air stops streaming in. *All the chairs are occupied*. The skulls from the graves are back in their old places. The windows are thickly curtained. Outside are moonshine and wind.

The chairs filled for a meeting. Muttering in the chairs. Silence in the chairs. The eternal matter of Sirius's Slaughterhouse:

> We are tired of the talk about dogs.
> We want no talk about dogs.
> What is all this talk about dogs?
> There never has been any dog.

Is there a smell of meat here?
Is a dog howling outside the wall?
Is this Sirius's Slaughterhouse?
Now it is the fourteenth night.

> There is no dog.
> *I say there is no dog.*
> Nor is there any Slaughterhouse.
> Why should there be a dog?
> There is no smell.
> No smell at all.

No dog exists.

It is howling beside a crack.
Night after night beside a crack.
A crack that cannot be caulked.
A crack and a dog?

> *There is no dog.*
> Sirius's Slaughterhouse—
> what is that?
> Such a thing has never
> existed.
> Sirius's Slaughterhouse—
> which of us is mad?
> I say there is no dog.

It howls on the seventh night,
howls on the fourteenth night,
beside a crack leading into

Sirius's Slaughterhouse.
Nightly the moon waxes larger.

There is no trace of a dog.
Not the slightest trace of a dog.

The moon has been sent to the earth
to shed light on all things.
Nightly the moon waxes larger,
shining longer,
shining stronger,
shining down its broad path.

As you know the moon is now at its zenith.
This very evening the moon will wane.
No dog has ever existed.
I say there is no dog.

Silence.

Silence?

The night passes and the storm moves on. From this evening the moon will wane. The skulls are back beneath the grass, lying in great peace. The night passes and passes, and from this evening the moon will wane.

Is there more?

The wind. Nothing else. The wind that will never drop.

At long last a clangour of copper: Clang – clang.

Morning.

Clang – clang.

THE MORNING AS REVELATION. The new day is reddening on the mountain peaks. A brand new day. Far above the rats, one might say, if one wanted to say such a thing.

And there was no day yesterday.

It has suddenly struck us. We are wise as after some wonderful liberation: there *was* no day yesterday.

That's how it goes when things go as they ought.

Everything is new. There was no day yesterday.

Clang – echoing copper strokes.

The skulls are resting peacefully beneath the grass. Inside the halls morning-pale women are washing the chairs clean as gold, for the day's meeting. Waves are lapping the embankments on all the shores.

SOMEONE IS IN PAIN. It did not happen here. Someone is dying. It did not happen here. It was a long way away – and it's not certain to be true. The world is large. The world contains such infinite variety – and we need not know more about it than that.

The chairs are waiting *here*. The rats are waiting in the cellar here. Small beetles are sending obscure signals here. Here we shave our chins and make ourselves smart and well-scented for important meetings.

The waves lap against the embankment from ocean to ocean.

The grass grows up and fades. The spring matures, the

graves flower. The autumns are cool and fine, they mature and fade. Beetles nibble at each other in the back. He who does not know this, knows nothing.

CLANG – CLANG.

Those copper strokes again.

They sound deep, rich, right.

Like everything.

We skulls recognize all confident copper voices. They report that the lines are straight and secure.

Clang – clang.

To the chairs. To the chairs.

To a completely new day.

Completely new – it dawned rosy as a virgin up among the peaks.

We process to the chairs. Our skulls tingle with the morning. Chairs clean as gold. A brand new day.

Washed Cheeks

A SOLITARY, THICK GROVE of leafy trees. And the loveliest weather. Warm rain that has a quality of great gentleness, a quality of deep peace.

It doesn't look as if there is anyone in the grove – although there are actually five men. It is much too quiet in there. Quiet has come to these five men for good.

But who are the five?

Nobody knows.

They are five soldiers, five completely strange soldiers who have been forgotten. They came here shooting or not shooting, came marching through this district together with countless others, but more to one side than the rest. It happened that way. They are very young. Most likely they were highly regarded.

That is irrelevant now. They are lying on the ground in different attitudes, and it is raining on them.

YES, THE MEN are lying on the ground and it is raining on them. They have not moved today nor did they yesterday. It rained on them calmly and peacefully both yesterday and today, the same quiet, warm rain that is raining now.

It rained during the night between the two days of rain as well. The days of rain were linked by a night of rain.

DURING LAST NIGHT, which was unexpectedly quiet after all that shattering hellish din, it rained on the five men in the darkness all the time. Early this morning their stiff cheeks were washed and white.

The color must be called white, but it is much closer and at the same time much further away than white; it has no human name.

Five men. That's not many.

One for each finger on your hand.

Practically nothing.

The rain is washing them.

TALK OF QUIET.

The night before last various sounds and cries came from this thick, leafy grove. Gradually, as the night wore on, it fell quiet there. One after the other had nothing more to groan about. There was no more to tell about the five, nor were there more than five of them.

That night was anything but quiet. The earth trembled and death mowed in wide swathes. The five men were furthest off to one side in an outpost, but death sought them there too. They did not fall quiet in a flash; they fell quiet eventually. Eventually. It has been raining since. They needed washing, so there seemed to be some order in it.

Nobody can understand what really happened that night and the preceding days, but it happened in a din that hounded all the animals and birds far, far away to other, quieter places. The five will not be found by animals or birds for a long time. Nor will they be found by people clearing up – for they have other things to do: new and bigger things are happening in new areas every day.

There was no time to search in all the outlying areas. A new great day is shaking the earth at this moment, but far away, and it demands all possible help there. There are many thousands. Here in the grove there are only five.

THOSE WHO ARE HERE now will remain here. They will never be identified. They are far from where anyone lives and anyone walks. And they are not in a friendly country. No one will organize big search parties. No one will find them except the flies. When the rain finally stops the flies will crawl out. The flies do not let themselves be frightened by cannon.

That's all there is to it, and no one in their own country knows anything about them. Missing in the storm. In the country far away someone is asking after them day and night. There they have their little circle of desperate friends. No use. The five simply vanished. No one has seen them.

Order? There must be some kind of grim order somewhere. What's the use of that?

Whiter and whiter the men's cheeks.

It's so simple. The rain streams down peacefully, and the cheeks lying on the ground are washed ceaselessly. The hands too. Their hands have clenched against something in the hour of extremity. The rain bleaches and cleans these hands too. It soaks them with soft rain water as if to open them, but they cannot be opened, cannot be made gentle. Even if they lie there until everything has blown away, they will not be made gentle. They will forever remain damning clenched fists.

THE TREES IN THE GROVE seem to lean closer together in this weather. They stand forming an extra screen of dew and mist. The low bushes, too, spread out even more widely in the rain, as if to close all openings.

The white cheeks form a disorderly heap.

Whiter and whiter, against what is coming: soon they will shine.

An incredible thought, but one that is playing here, waiting.

There is opposition somewhere: No, no, don't shine!

Is there no blind order in such matters?

Senseless order, but order. Do not shine. There must be some order that can stop whatever becomes too difficult to accept.

There is certainly order. When matters have come as far as this, then grim order begins. When it is too late. When the storm has passed on, to cause more pale cheeks – then an order that is too late can come to the five lonely men in the grove.

But yet again: the stakes are high.

This is the number five.

What does five mean in such stakes?

It does not mean so much as a jerk in a commanding eyebrow, far less any reason for a dirge.

It means less than a mote in the eye, in the right place. If the number were one hundred times five, or a thousand – the stakes are high, as we said. And the game must be played. Among glittering stars down on earth it will be said that the stakes are high and must be regarded as high.

What does five mean then?

The fingers on one hand, if you count like that.

For each of them being alive meant everything. Being included. Being a reason for existence together with the others. The groves lean in the rain, the five will be washed until they shine. No less than five times it meant everything.

THEY BECOME WHITER and whiter. They are nearing an eruption of light that is gaining ground.

They are washed all the day long. At the same time the grove seems to become denser. Another night is being made ready. The darkness will be sufficiently dense in there, as it must and shall. Such things must not lie in the half-dark. There is strict order – however late it may come.

During this third night the polishing is finished.

On the third night it begins.

Slowly, slowly the five faces begin to shine.

IN DENSEST NIGHT, while the warm, friendly rain continues unceasingly, bleaching in its gentle way –

then this other thing is ready and erupts, without any gentleness.

The trees do not stir. There is no wind. No animals are padding about either; the storm of death has chased them away. Only grass and leaves, and grass and leaves show no surprise that this is happening: a growing gleam of light from the five.

Their faces appear dimly out of the pitch blackness.

A clear, calm gleam. No flickering. Cheeks that have been washed until they triumph over the darkness, not by the rain but by other things, washed inwards to where they *must* shine. Silently and steadfastly like deep sorrow.

It is good that there are no people in this area. An ordinary person would not be able to bear it. This light is for those who are behind this cycle of events.

Now there is turmoil in the night. The darkness strides silently along. The grove shrinks to enfold what man brings about, yet cannot endure.

The music in the night – where is it? The rain continues. The gleam becomes stronger, more perilous. A dimly decaying gleam. There are a hundred thousand other places – this concerns only five. They are beginning to shine now.

Beginning to shine in the dark. Tomorrow the rain is likely to stop, and then the black flies will come. Now it is night and no fly dare come out.

THE GLEAM IS STRONGER already. Unwavering. The faces acquire it from unknown sources. The afterglow of crimes that rises up to heaven.

A gleam that draws and attracts and creates confusion and movement. In the grove where all life seems extinguished, there is now nothing but movement.

The darkness comes alive, is full of tiny life. The gleam awakens all minute sleeping creatures within reach. They come creeping out, infinitely small, but with the ability to notice anything unusual, moving jerkily towards the gleam in close formation. Attracted by it and lost by it: in that light they will vanish like dew.

Five faces are shining with the increasing strength of decay. Sharp rays that will be stopped by nothing. They pass through trees, through stones, through everything, lit by the need of innocent men.

The small voiceless creatures crawl towards them. They crawl out of their night to become witnesses. Secret voiceless witnesses.

WHAT OF ITS ERUPTING?
It had to come.
Tonight they are shining.

It had to come like that. There is order, though late. The tortured faces began to shine and it is a perilous light. It will be talked about late, but this order is late.

The rain is about to taper off. Tomorrow is the day for all the flies.

The destroyed faces are shining, and it is impossible to describe. It is not what one calls light. The creeping things vanish before it, as smoke vanishes. Torture vanishes too, at last.

What has happened tonight will never be made known. The millstones sink with their load to the bottom of the sea.

If a five-fold light were to shine afterwards through earth and trees and stones? Nothing. It will never be made known.

The decaying gleam is there only tonight. It will never be made known.

Fire in the Depths

THE ROAD THAT WINDS up the mountainside is deserted, no life there at all. No sound to be heard either. Nothing but stone and persistent sunshine. In the gashes in the rock stand a few hardy trees, their dry knuckles exposed, beside old, stunted bushes.

The heat comes from the steep walls of rock, which rise straight up from the roadway on the inner side. The sunshine is splintered against this wall and magnified by it.

On the outer side of the road there is nothing but blue air hanging in a heat haze above a deep valley far below. That's where the people are, that's where there's life and movement. No one travels up here on this mountain road any more.

This abandoned road in the mountain was blasted out with poor tools and much toil once upon a time; now it is useless and forgotten. The wound in the mountainside has darkened: in the cuts you can no longer see so clearly the boundaries of the ages, endless stone ages. It all hides itself beneath complicated patterns of moss and a common surface color. The large crevices in the rock, left after the upheavals of other epochs, have through the millennia been blown full of dust and seeds. Fertile soil for bushes and tussocks of grass. Dynamited masses of stone that tumbled downwards during the building of the road are now darkening scree at the foot of the mountain far below, overgrown with eager woods and thick layers of dead leaves.

FROM A CREVICE somewhere in the rock wall, about twice the height of a man above the road, there hangs a faded loop, as if placed there for pulling oneself up through the clefts in the stone. The loop hangs there all the time, but no one comes to grasp it. The slack noose hangs and hangs. No one has looked to see whether it is there day and night and forever. It must be, for it is always hanging in the same way. If a strong mountain wind is blowing one day it swings a little in the gust, just as any rope would do.

The slack, slightly withered noose or loop fits in with the rest of the unchanging scene, hanging there as if by chance.

To be grasped?

No, no one has done that. There is *life* in the rope. It is a part of something. The rest of the splendid serpent is hidden among the stones.

There is something about this that makes one reply instead: Nothing has been said about it.

Nobody knows of anyone who has tried to grasp it.

THE ROAD LEADS to a deserted valley. Once many people lived there, but life was more strenuous than in other places, and so one by one they went away. The last one left long ago, and the houses that stood there have disappeared. So no one returns. No one has any business there. So the road falls into disrepair. Eternally patient the loop hangs from the crevice. To be grasped. As if waiting for a long time – perhaps, all the same, someone will. A man cannot explain what kind of patience this is.

And men do not walk here.

Living things that look dead are avoided by men because they feel a numbness in themselves at the sight. A man is not like that. A man's blood is warm, his thoughts leaping and wild; and stubborn and impatient too. A normal man is a bird among birds, with the bird's unexpected plunge, and with the bird's wall-breaching song in his throat.

And what is this?

A loop.

Waiting year out and year in for someone to grasp it. Not a comfortable state of affairs.

But patience gets its reward.

AT LAST A REWARD.

At last a man on the road.

Such unbelievable, cold patience has not been waiting for nothing. A man will come here. What more he will do is his own affair when he arrives.

There are many bends and turns on this road. The man has just started on the very first of them. How far up will he walk? But he is walking quickly so far – considering how steep the road is and how hot the day. It looks as if some strong incentive is driving him on.

What does he want?

He is a man with the heart of a bird. It is fitting that he should be walking here above dizzy heights, with the blue air beneath him.

He is just walking. He rounds another bend. The ascent and the sunshine make him breathe heavily. He is not a bird in everything.

He seems to be pushed forward by his own hot breath, on this road where nobody walks. It is good enough testimony that he is on the road at all. He is searching for something. It looks as if he is driven to it.

He is already beginning to peer upwards along the steep walls of rock to his left. He never crosses over to the other side of the road, although the most beautiful view is to be had from there. He does not look down into the valley. He looks quickly and searchingly at every new chunk of rock that comes into view as he rounds the bends. He is obviously expecting to find someone.

How has he found out about it? No one is likely to have told him.

He is a young man.

There's *that* too. A young man.

Curious not to go over to the edge where the view is, and the freedom puts flight into one's brain. Instead he scans the confining rock wall where it is difficult to breathe and the sun's heat is burning.

So he must know about something that is irresistible to someone like himself.

The one bend after the other. Irresistible. He has a young heart, which cannot find rest. All it can do is search, and never mind about the result. The heat from the walls meets his own burning urge to walk, and to walk fast. He does not pause, scanning the walls as he walks.

Perhaps he knows about something and is afraid of it, but must see it, must find it. And find it alone. He walks like one who is very much alone.

A delicate trickling meets his ear as he rounds a bend. He starts in surprise at first, but there is no cause for alarm, it *is* water, trickling right out of the rock and down into a mossgrown horse trough hewn out of stone.

A memento of time past. The water still trickles out of the stone, from a vein that never dries up, still cold in the extreme heat. A welcome sight. The man looks round him before bending down to drink. In the trough he encounters his own face and avoids looking at it, drinking the refreshing mountain water quickly and walking on.

He looks with the same suspense as before at everything along the roadside. There is not much to see. He walks like a tired, frightened boy, but with the bird's heart, which he cannot help having.

Bend after bend.

The sun strikes his back. Utter stillness. The scraping of his footsteps in the gravel the only sound.

And then he is there.

The bends have become sharper. In his suspense he has not noticed.

SHARPER – so that he comes on the thing all of a sudden. It is the loop. The dead noose hanging from the crevice. Right in front of him all of a sudden. Twice the height of a man up the rock wall. It resembles a tree-root that has looped itself unexpectedly in the air, and then turned and crawled in again.

The young man looks at it. It does not seem important hanging there. A loop like that hanging without reason, in burning sun. But he does not move a muscle, so fascinated is he. Unable to take his eyes off it.

He knew about it all the time. Here it is, and now matters must take their course.

Something is happening, unseen. And there is no name for it. An encounter between the young man and this object in the rock that looks like a loop. An encounter between what he possesses himself and what has been biding its time here, and is ready to meet him now.

He stands still as they meet.

No, they are not meeting yet, they have not come so far. This is only an initiation, an opening.

He receives images of things he did not know about, and hints of things over which he has no control, being uncertain about their limits.

The bird in him brings this about perhaps, though it does not seem to have much to do with birds.

The loop does not move and the young man stands stock-still in front of it. He must be thinking, startled: So it was this.

But that it should be like this?

And that it must be like this?

I don't think I will.

He thinks this in the small space he has left to move in. The two that are to meet in him are beginning to fill it up.

He looks at the loop a little longer, and then he says: I will.

He only says it for the sake of saying it. He knows there is only one thing to do: He must do it.

Should he go over and press his forehead against it? Is that all that must be done?

No, no, he thinks.

But he will. He thinks: *That it should be like this!*

I can't, he thinks.

He has to think all this for the sake of appearances. The moment he saw the loop hanging there he knew what he had to do. It is futile to pretend to push it aside. In a while he is ready. He will and he can scramble up and take hold of the loop. He will soon find out what happens afterwards.

I shan't get up there, the rock is smooth.

He knows very well that he will get up. This is fate – and he is the helpless heart of a bird that has let itself be lured.

Smooth rock. Impossible to get up there without special equipment. No sooner has he thought this than he looks more carefully, and sees good handholds and footholds in the twelve feet he needs. Does he know what he is nearing? No way round it.

No way round – had he thought there *was*? Something in him wants to run away.

No, he says sharply.

It's too late anyway. He is really hanging already on the rock wall like a fly.

The loop still hangs motionless above his head. He is half-way up to it, and it is no problem to climb the rest of the way, but still he pauses. As if to show that he can do *that*.

That I can make some decisions myself.

Then he crawls the last short stretch, using the safe footholds. Then his bare forehead is on a level with the loop.

Ugh, with my forehead.

Why not?

Precisely with my forehead.

With his hands he clings to the rock. His hands are trembling. The brown, or brownish-black, loop is just in front of his eyes. Then he does it: he touches the loop cautiously with his forehead.

The loop gives a tiny jerk.

Then there is nothing more, then the loop seems dead again.

It almost makes him fall from the cleft he is standing in. Fire runs through him. The first. There will be no more. He seizes the edge of a crevice and saves himself.

If he had expected something cold it had turned out otherwise. The loop was as mild as the air it hung in, warmed by the sun like everything else. But it was not a dead thing. Against his forehead he had felt the tiny, sudden jerk of life. What kind of life?

In a flash there was a meeting. The two that met in him have settled side by side and have started to burn.

He cannot move a finger. He is here now. Before him hangs the loop. Should he grasp it, since it was made to be grasped? No no. He is tempted to do so, to let go with his right hand and clutch at the thick loop. No no.

A cautious grip would be impossible, he is so dazed. A clutch. What would happen?

Impossible to tell, but what *has* happened would be destroyed. Why don't you get away?

I can't.

Neither of them move. Nothing seems to be happening. Things did happen in a flash before they began burning. From the one to the other and back again.

The loop does not begin to glide, does not haul itself up or down, there is no more to be seen of it than is there already. There is no one here who can look into the young man's eyes to see if they are dead. If that's what has happened. He has not moved a muscle. Is he going to stand here forever, like the other? Does he no longer exist?

Minutes pass perhaps. No one is counting them. Everything has turned to stone.

Dead? Oh no. Rushing rivers move towards the unknown. One understands it, one knows it, even when turned to stone. Towards the unknown. Rivers. If he should become anything after this, he will never be the same as before.

He relaxes his muscles at last. His body loses the tension that was turning him to stone. He opens his mouth, but checks what he was about to say. His fingers, itching with the desire to grasp the rope, fumble for crevices to bear him during the climb down. His hands change handholds, his feet change clefts for standing in. Then there are no clefts, and he slides down the last little stub of smooth rock to the road.

Above him hangs the loop as before. No difference in colour or shape.

THE FIRE IS RAGING in the young man. A fire in the depths. And experiences have passed through him like dark logs on the rivers. They are still doing so.

He is back on the old, neglected road in front of the

rock with the loop. He makes no attempt to look up at it. Shrinking from it, he walks instead across the road, out to the edge above the giddy precipice. There is a blue haze downwards and outwards. Far below he can see a cluster of human dwellings on the bank of a foaming river. He is looking straight down at the roofs of the houses. He sees cars speeding along the highway like small beetles. He sees people walking without moving from the spot, tiny as ants.

He looks at it thirstily. He is thirsty for it at this moment. He has become so now. At this moment, now that something seems to have been moved out of the way. When the thought passed through him that the way ahead was open.

The rivers passed into the unknown. He knows no more than that. He has found no certainty. He stands at the outermost edge of the road, where the warm gusts of heavy valley air dance towards him from the slopes below.

Standing and standing. It is a different person standing here. Different in a flash. Different because of things one refuses to think about. Fire in the depths.

There had been fire before. That was what had driven him upwards, that had brought about the encounter. Fire met fire. Then the way became open. It cannot be explained, it's a riddle, but the way is somehow open in the daze.

Burnt and free, is that what he is? He stands looking down into the valley at the others. There they are, side by side. At his wit's end he stands looking down at them. On fire. The way open.

What is this open way buzzing around him? He cannot shout about it to the people down there, if he does go back to them in a while. The things he must say are spoken silently to himself for lack of courage.

He was driven into this, afraid, but going straight towards it. Now he suddenly feels lonely.

Side by side – does it mean that I can never experience *that* any more after this?

Was *that* what burnt up?

THE HOT ROCK STANDS, housing and hushing up secrets, the things a young person feels in himself and longs for. He who rushes away, burnt and giddy, has nothing to tell. We met and caught fire – such things cannot be told, for fear of ridicule.

It is his fire, but he has become lonely. He did not know this. Lonely in an instant maybe.

There are the shadows and the ascents and the rock crevices and the hiding places. And what one does not name. There are the graves too, for the things no one knows, when what can happen up in the mountain is already accomplished. He who stands thus does not shout about these things; he must not after the fire in the depths. Perhaps he may some time, but not now. He stands repeating to himself with trembling voice: Met and caught fire.

What did meet is hidden from the man who stands here trembling.

SIDE BY SIDE.

One must be side by side.

Certainly not in order to talk about it. Absolutely nothing must be told. But to avoid the loneliness after the fire.

What was that about the open way? Was it a moment of fantasy?

The winds from the valley rise in gusts against his face, from the dells, from the banks, from the knolls below. Beneath flows the river in bright waterfalls at night, while people pass into the night and think no more. He stands up on the road, looking down. Do they remember how quickly it can change? The next morning the snow of death may be lying on the peaks.

Suddenly he looks thirstily for people. They are moving about below. He must go down.

What will happen then?

Happen? he asks himself, afraid.

After a while he has recovered sufficiently from the strain to begin the walk downhill. He soon feels better. Better the further down he goes.

Soon he will be walking alongside the river. The river flows quite fast down the steep valley, but without much volume at this time of year. Up at the bend in the road he played with the idea of the shining river flowing through the summer night. He only did it for pleasure and because he needed to. No waterfall can shine now.

Down to people now.

What will happen?

A SULTRY SUMMER'S DAY. He has come down to the highway and there are people on both sides of it. Most of them are busy in the fields and do not notice him as he passes by. A stream of people are speeding past in their cars. He looks for someone who is not busy, and catches sight of a figure sitting in the grass in a garden a short distance from the road. Without hesitation he turns off the road and goes straight towards her. It is a young girl sitting in the hot sunshine.

A girl, of course.

He does not know her very well, but is aware of who she is. He has talked to her casually once or twice.

She sits in the grass, attractive in a thin summer dress, her healthy skin glowing through it. She gets to her feet before he reaches her. Why does she do that? Is she afraid of him?

He sees she is uneasy.

"Good day."

"Good day?" she replies, clearly in the form of a question.

"No, it was nothing," he says quickly, and stops short.

"No, of course not. Why should there be anything?" she says. But she has begun to look at him.

Look at him? Yes, look at him. He is uneasy himself, and notices it.

He says quickly, "I saw you were sitting in the grass. Is anything the matter?"

"Surely I'm the one who ought to ask that," she answers his eyes, but she does not sound as if she is repulsing him.

"Am I intruding?"

"Why should I think that?" she asks his eyes. "You must have some errand here."

Has he an errand? He has an errand that makes him tremble. What can she read in him? She asks abruptly, as if it dropped out of her mouth: "What is it?"

"No," he says, cutting it off.

In a little while he says. "There's something else I'd like to say."

"Oh?" she says to his eyes.

"That I like you."

"No."

She is blushing.

"You don't mean that," he says.

She is silent to his eyes.

"You don't mean it, do you?" he says.

"Run away, then," he says, trembling in case she takes him seriously. He looks at her forehead, he sees only her forehead that is free and beautiful.

She does not run away. He understands that she has no intention of running away. He stares at her forehead as if parched with thirst.

"You're the first person I've met," he tells her. It sounds stupid to anyone who has not been with him.

"What do you mean?"

"Never mind. Don't you want to sit down again?"

She does not take her eyes off him. She says: "I'll stand as long as you're standing."

He gives a start. But he does not say: All right, *I'll* sit down then. He stands looking at her forehead. One of them must have taken a step forward, for they are close to each other. He is aware of the fragrance rising from her dress. I am among people, I am among people, he thinks.

He sees she wants to come closer. She has no idea what has been happening.

"May I ask you something?" he asks.

"I don't know," she answers his eyes.

"I suppose you can tell me what it is," she says again. Her eyes have changed. They keep changing.

"Your forehead," he says, stupidly.

"What do you mean, my forehead? You're so strange today. I've never seen you like this before."

He nods.

Her forehead is just in front of him. He puts his arms round her shoulders. There are only a couple of narrow straps across them. He tilts her head towards him slightly so that her forehead is projecting. Numb with tension he places his own forehead gently against hers.

She flinches as if he were burning hot.

"Ouch, let go!"

Disappointment engulfs him like an avalanche. It had not freed him; it had not gone away. But the other: dark logs and rivers swirling away into the unknown.

"What did you say?" he asks afraid. She does not answer.

He has already released her. His arms are hanging down. His eyes are staring at her in fright.

"Go on, run," he says.

She does not run. She takes a step backwards, and stays there – in a silence that is difficult to bear. She does not take her eyes off him.

She tells him: "I didn't mean it."

She takes two steps forward, straight towards him. Her eyes are blurred and heavy.

"My dear," she says.

A dark roaring towards the unknown. Logs and rivers....

"What is it?"

"I want to kiss you," she says with open mouth.

He says indistinctly, in the frightening unknown: "You don't know what you're kissing."

"I want to kiss you just the same."

Words, Words

HE THOUGHT OF EVERYTHING that might have happened, but never came so far.

Because it was stopped by someone who was on guard when matters became really serious, but a warning that was always trustworthy.

So one did not fall into the traps; one could return to one's own place.

A clear eye that understood what was important. That could calmly allow this to happen and that to happen, but put a stop to such activity when there was real danger.

This has been recorded on a tablet.

One can bring out one's tablet now and then. There all that should have been said through the time of silence is written down. A time which was also the time of long comradeship.

NOW, THIS WAS *ONE* CONSIDERATION. And a basic one. But there were others.

He could sit and think like this: What about the candid generosity that put him in his place when something or other had been done too meanly? How could he react in such a situation?

Feel ashamed and turn aside. Keep away for a while in anger. Take offense.

Keep away, and give unjust anger and offended looks time, in order to let them fade finally in bitter acknowledgment of the truth. Come out again after a while, incapable of saying anything, only passing slowly by and perhaps pausing for a little, standing there for a little.

She would have understood.

No one mentioned the matter. One's tongue was useless just then.

Words can cause trouble like large rocks in one's path.

Wrong: Words can clear the largest rocks out of the way.

Wrong again: Words can turn into dark chasms unbridgeable for a whole lifetime.

We know very little about the power and the destructiveness of words.

IT'S AS IF THERE WERE NOTHING MORE – when one has brought out the tablet.

But what about the person who was always there when needed? Always willingly beside you? Important as bread is important and as indispensable.

He said to himself: Perhaps that's what I must remember more often. But did I ever speak about what I really knew? Far too difficult. Far too extraordinary to be blurted out in words.

Nor did he remember everything. Too many years. And there was much that could not be brought out into the open. Certain matters are best left like that.

He thought: One says far too many stupid, awkward things. Most often they are awkward. The things one says usually seem to be left lying about on the floor like a pair of lop-sided shoes – while the things one wanted to say feel like birds in flight.

To keep silent about matters of importance is not just modesty. One's wretched tongue is wooden. Small matters are chattered about, blurted out. One keeps silent about the rest until it is perhaps forgotten and lying in various graves.

What should he be called, then, he who is responsible for this?

AS IF THERE WERE NOTHING MORE.

He thought sometimes, to comfort himself: I have it. It has not gone. All this has been carved in vivid letters on that tablet.

Well, bring it out.

That tablet will never be brought out. It is a tablet no one may read, no one may see.

So it exists only in the imagination, I suppose.

It exists.

What's the use, if it's not meant for anyone.

It feels as if it's some use to me, at any rate. And, as I said, the tablet is there.

As if there were nothing more than this. I could sit at

supper remembering new things. They would appear from their graves all the same.

He thought and thought.

HE THOUGHT: Words, words.

No more words now.

Here is my thirsting hand.

The Dream of Stone

BETWEEN THE WALLS OF STONE – and there it is better to be alone, they tell you as you are let in to their dense, leaden dream.

I don't understand. Stone walls, what business have I there? What have I to do between the stone walls?

The answer comes: That is a reasonable question.

Only afterwards does it dawn on you.

NO FURTHER EXPLANATION of how you have arrived between these stone walls. These smooth rocks that stand so defiantly upright. Suddenly you are there, that is all you know.

Between smooth, sun-warmed stone walls, and between stone mouths that certainly exist, but are not visible.

You think of the mouths. Then you have entered.

The rock here is not cold. Accumulated sun. The walls are like the sides of an oven. The heat from the walls is like the gentle strokes of a club on the back of your neck. No one would come here of his own accord; I dare not find out why I am here myself.

But it's the stone mouths.

If only the stone mouths would open and tell me what I am seeking. But the stone must return to its stone and it is not likely to help me. There is really nothing besides burning walls of rock and astonishment.

Say something, mouth.

One stands stock-still in bewilderment at the sight: smooth, steep stone walls. Closed. Fathomlessly silent.

But one prays: Say something, mouth.

Not the slightest sign of an answer.

These are upright stone plateaux. Steep and gentle by turns. They lean over dangerously as well, you feel their proximity if you doze off. But no mouth.

For the third time: Say something, mouth.

I am sure there is a mouth deep in the stone, but the stone must return to its stone and cannot reveal itself. Do I see this? Where am I?

WHERE ARE MY CLOTHES?

Time does not exist. It rose up like vapor as one turned round and looked for it. I have stripped long ago in this scorching heat. I prayed three times: Speak! But no mouth is open. You become uneasy and expect violence. Then your own concerns are not enough.

Smooth rock facing south, and long periods of burning sun. The stone has absorbed it all and is breathing out again. Hot flagstones burn the soles of my feet. They are too hot to walk on when you are completely naked.

I believe that these great expanses of stone have echoing cries within them. The cries are silent within the walls. They thud on the back of one's neck if one goes close. One thinks of all the rock walls one has ever seen. Sometimes they plunge steeply into lakes and seas, fissured from thousand-year-old bolts of lightning. Sometimes they plunge vertically down into the quagmires, and from there they will probably cry out one day with crushing horror about the time of the rock in the quagmires. It will certainly be terrible to hear.

It is already the time of bewilderment, so that one forgets

oneself and says, believing it to be of use: Say something, mouth.

Oh no.

But one is standing here, caught in all this heat that has accumulated in these upright surfaces. A little fever murmurs somewhere in the seeker who has come and does not quite know how to start.

One may walk naked for the sake of love – a few words that come to mind because I am walking like this, but they are inappropriate here, in loneliness between scraped rocks. I am naked and do not understand. But it is good to walk beside these warm stone walls. I opened my eyes and was there. Walking with a little fever in an abode of stone.

Yet another abode of stone.

WILL THE SEALED MOUTHS explain the truth about these abodes of stone, or will they remain, here as elsewhere, silent?

Or shall I go on walking here until finally I walk *into* the stone and stand there as if sealed? A mouth without redemption. Then others will come, confused by the heat and the strokes of the club, and say something to each other as they are shut in, that I do not understand. Fever-hot smooth rock, what is happening to me and to others?

I stand inside the stone without a mouth, and the others have to leave. They asked their question and left.

Is there more?

No, there's nothing to start on. One sees only oneself in the stone. There everything is sealed, yet one sees oneself in the stone exactly as created, and walks quickly past oneself with beating heart. The walls in the rock are smooth yet deeply troubled.

The stone closes up and is alive without a face. Is alive so that one trembles in there, and then the sides begin leaning forward and turn threatening.

Can nothing be said to one who has not yet been given a valid answer; who has been to many places and asked, and who has come back none the wiser?

It has grown late, silent stone mouths. And I do not mean late in time.

THE ROCK THAT PLUNGES vertically down into the quagmires, think of that. Down into the dark depths of the quagmires. Down until it meets rock from the other side. There it must remain. A strange meeting. Moss grows on a small section of the rock up in the light of day.

Vertically down into the quagmires.

THERE!

Unexpectedly it starts to rain in the middle of this heat. A cloud has moved in during the past few minutes and begun to shade the sun. An eager cloud full of rain. From its outermost fringes it is already letting fall a few large, lukewarm drops. Towards the centre the cloud is threateningly blue.

And now there is a sudden change. The first drops fall like small explosions on the hot surface of the stone, followed at once by tremendous turmoil. The flung drops are unusually large, and they are given a special reception.

THEY STRIKE AGAINST THE STONE and are turned into specks of vapour which spread in the air into lazy puffs of pent-up desires. They rise from the hard surface as if from deep sleep. Lazy puffs of breath from the stone mouth.

The puffs come in quick succession as the drops splash and lick, as more surfaces and walls and flagstones are included and send out their fragrance and their smell and their stink. Whether one wants it or not, the breaths advance towards one, pressing forward from all kinds of hidden places and mingling together.

With pounding pulse one becomes a part of it.

The vapour blows in gusts against one's body. One stands naked; this is for the naked and for nobody. It makes one giddy in an instant.

Breathing and smells from all sides. The strongest is the smell that is so shut in, elemental and savage. My back feels chilled, but not from uneasiness; these are deep shudders of what I was longing for. The stone mouths must be open somewhere. This is a salutation from within the walls.

It seems important to move about and receive fresh salutations from the puffs of vapor; to find new pettiness, new ways of handling pettiness and stupidity, and what is larger, and what is too large.

The smell flows more densely, without becoming rank; it is muted and strange, like the dream, and like one's use of something unfamiliar. As sleep is creative and renewing, so the senses are there to be sharpened – by standing naked, aware of the flaws in oneself. Aware of the abyss and ready to collapse, and nobody can say a truly comforting word about this, or explain it.

The stone has acquired life.

Quicker than it can be told, at breakneck speed, in a few angry seconds it all happens. But the stone mouths have not opened; the rain from outside has woken them. The walls are ready to be shattered by what is shut in. Life rages in the tensions constrained in the spectacle before one's eyes. One stands in the middle of it, naked as never before, aware of the rock leaning over, threatening with closed mouth.

One stands there, imagining that the stone is ready to crack open because it is alive. The stone's breath bewitches a man so that he sees stone surfaces rise up and remain standing as walls and tilting towers.

DO WE REALLY SEE IT?

Yes, when we *want* to see it.

What is the truth about our senses? Do we sense so much as a thousandth part?

One tries to take part in everything as much as possible, in order to come closer. The scattered raindrops lick the stone and sustain its agitation, and my own agitation comes from being able to stand in the middle of this – to feel them mingling and becoming twice as strong. One can sense it without being annihilated oneself. All the same it passes from the one to the other and turns into some kind of silent avowal, powerful and threatening because it cannot be grasped.

No sooner is this established than I realize I have eyes in the back of my neck: I can see simultaneously in all directions in the bewitching vapour. Is it because I cannot bear to admit that my strength is borrowed? Because of it I have eyes in the back of my neck. I see the rock rise upwards like towers with battlements wreathed in green, some upright, others leaning and ready to fall. And they begin to move, nodding their crowns of rock like treetops on a stormy ridge. This I see with the back of my neck.

Something must come of this, and it turns out to be a melody. A chorus. The deepest notes in a chorus. But no dirge. We do not talk about going away. We do not talk at all, we are sonorous and towering choruses.

At once I feel that I am one with them. The smooth side is now outside me. I am not astonished, it is exactly as it should be. This is where one must enter and join in the chorus. Man belongs to the choir, but enters through his own perplexity.

OUR GREAT CHOIR moves outwards.

The senses simultaneously acute and numb. The song that is outside man. Tremendous, and soundless. Rocks that rise on end, and are given breath and the faculty of song for the small space of time when they are allowed to take part. I myself am given the faculty of song and can take part in the chorus. It will never happen again. Perhaps it is a warning, but one does not think about that. It is important to take part until the breaking point.

As if hewn into the stone it is also laid down that this must soon rupture and disintegrate.

IN CHORUS WE SING of the stone. Of the rock in the quagmire. Of endless, mute aeons. Of the unfailing strength of the rock, which is on the point of erupting all the time. We sing of the waiting of the rock, and again of endless aeons. I raise my voice with them, and sing of man's brief and pitiful confusion, of man's pitiful life. The rock takes part too, singing sonorously the song of sorrow about man's brief span.

NO – ONE IS FORCED TO THINK mutely from within the mighty choir – it is not quite true about man's pitiful life. Man's life is not always pitiful. It can be as manifold as the glitter in a waterfall. It is the song of the rock that leads one astray.

The choir takes no notice of such matters. Rocks that have risen up and flexed themselves into towers merely proceed. A choir of mountain sides. We sing on, we sing of those which lean to the dangerous side, yet stand. Stand leaning and collecting shadows. We include rocks we have never seen. We include everything about rock and stone and quag-mires, and yet it feels as if we are thin membranes, ready to rupture. We sing of each other. We sing of great mouths in stone.

THIS UNIMAGINABLE CHOIR of stone mouths and battlements – can it hold out?

Don't think. A choir like this does not think.

One gives oneself up to it as if prompted by deep desire, letting the song of the rock become one's own, whether there is sense in it or not. One takes part while there is still time, while everything is dizzily precious and time is short.

Don't think. The tops of the towers each have their own wind, they are bent each in its own path, criss-crossing like scissors. One knows one does not see it, yet sees it. One is naked and one is nothing, but may take part in the chorus, while the rock opens its heavy stone chambers.

As I sing I nervously expect the song to die away after a

while. The old wish: Say something, mouth, has been granted a jarring fulfilment.

But it is the hour.

No no.

It is the hour. It suddenly grows dark as if a wall were falling.

Straight above.

Transfixed, I watch the battlements. Cracked asunder at the summit. Liberated. An avalanche is falling from the liberated summit.

No, it is no falling wall, it is the twilight from the dark cloud which is sinking slowly downwards. The twilight that came with the sudden downpour. Now it is moving in. A cloud hanging low with rain from the summits of rock.

Moving in.

Chorus and wildness. Seconds and swaying slopes. The tension. The burning walls of rock. Nothing. Then the downpour came, cooling and quenching.

The bold spectacle may not be driven further. Unbroken threads of water are already striking with their wet, deliberate force. What dwelt in the rock will be driven inwards. The rain pours down the smooth walls, cooling, quenching and flowing. The chorus is silent, as all stone is silent.

The tumult of the scissoring battlements is over. There is only one leaning wall here – and under it stands a man, naked and alone, shivering in the rain, awakened yet again.

No use listening for choirs in the tops of the towers when it is pouring like this.

Wet is wet, and the smell of wet. No seducing vapor. Naked in the rain and the wet. The stone has returned to its stone.

The Heart Lies Naked Beside the Highway in the Dark

THE MOON HAS REACHED its narrowest phase; its light is no longer of use. Thick darkness surrounds the house. A long dark evening will stride ahead – stride into an even thicker pall. Downwards and downwards, thicker and thicker.

If there is a heart here, it is lonely. The heart grows lonely; that is how it was created. It grows finally into its true self.

Lonely. It is far to its neighbor, and there it is a stranger. So it has even further to go.

The house grows lonely too. Its daytime character is of no importance now. Now there are other laws and other highways, other waterways. If there were lighted window panes within reach up to today, this is no longer true. The lighted panes have vanished and are of no consequence.

Is there no order here?

Increasingly so.

Where light gleamed, and then was extinguished, there everything was in order. The panes vanished and the eyelids closed peacefully. Quiet ticking, and then sleep. Lamp after lamp now signify sleep upon sleep. Order reigns according to its own rules.

But a lonely heart is not safe in the house. It has only itself, perhaps not even that. In the approaching night this cannot be counted on.

Do we not own our hearts in the end?

We know very little about it. That is one of the many uncertainties in life.

Tonight nothing is certain. That is why you have not shut your eyes.

I must have certainty.

The reply comes: Can't you see that your heart is lying naked on the highway, exhibiting itself there of its own accord? You know it well, but you try to hide your knowledge.

Since one is a little tired one has to answer: it is true.

It is true that my heart lies naked on or beside the highway when it is dark. It is not the first evening it has happened.

It is waiting for someone. It goes out and lies down at the roadside, trembling with boldness. At night it can do things like that. Nobody else is embarrassed by it and nobody will feel he has to ask questions.

In the darkness when everything is unknown.

How it will end is the tension of each night. There is no way of stopping this.

In the daytime this is the crossroads of the world. At night the thoroughfares are innumerable; they are nothing and everything. It is no use thinking that the four thoroughfares start here, as if one lay at the dead centre of the highways, at the point of departure. No, I have halted here and bared my heart because I could come no further. I was really in the house all the time.

Naked beside the unknown road at night.

Why naked? Why that word exactly?

Because it feels like that. Clothes are not very important in the dark.

Defenseless?

That too. The feeling, at any rate.

But with a blind need to be there. To face what is coming

towards me along the road. And stand defenseless just when one should defend oneself. Is that logical?

Nobody has said that one can defend oneself. One is simply naked in the darkness. One has to take that risk, to lie stripped beside the highway where the traffic is heavy.

The highway goes straight forward through the darkness, but it is no use asking about anything. And you will not be given any information. You will be expected to show courage and say nothing.

You really wanted to say in wild defiance: Just you come!

You will not say it. One weaves such fantasies, knowing one will never dare, never bring oneself to do it.

NOBODY CALLED and nobody came.

My heart is in its chamber, lying beside the road and lying in the house beside the road at the same time. The one does not preclude the other. My heart is thudding against the walls. Is it certain that nothing will happen tonight?

I don't know.

In any case this is *one night more at the roadside*.

And what was *that*?

A thudding against the wall.

My heart pauses slightly, in its great tension. It was the soft thudding of wood against wood outside. The gentle thud of a boat butting the wall in a wind. Can this be true?

Is there suddenly a sea out there? And a moored boat butting the wall of the house?

Butting the wall of the house in a storm. What storm? Moored to the wall and running into the wall, in a storm.

There's no boat outside. Not even water enough for a boat, it's a garden out there.

Garden?

How does one know what may be outside on a night like this? There may be an endless ocean. There may be a quay for the boat. In that case a shallow little boat could be lying waiting.

The nightlight is burning, one sees everything on the other side of the wall: the boat running into the posts in the wind; the boat that is tied to the ring and sometimes does not reach the post at all, but the wall. One has heard a good deal of that kind of thudding, and hears at once that this sound is a thousand miles removed from it.

Tied to the ring in the wall of my house. Where there has never been water and never any boat or ring. Now the boat is thudding against the wall in a storm.

Very well. One does not ask questions, one simply notes the fact. That's how it is beside the highway.

But the heart suddenly feels that it is getting more cramped. This is happening beside the unknown highway – so, land or sea, does it matter? Not in the least. The sea goes up on land at night so that the boat can be tied to the ring. The worn heart senses clearly that the boat is tied close by.

COME TO THAT, there may be moorings all round the house. Mooring is a pleasant word. Who dares draw himself to his full height and deny that the sea goes up on land and moors the boat to the ring during the dark nights? Who dares deny that such a storm exists? Who dares sneer and say that it is a good friend knocking?

One is out beside the great thoroughfare, where everything is possible. The assertions line up. One cannot bring oneself to utter them, but lets them live.

CANNOT BRING ONESELF to utter it aloud. My heart has already begun beating again. What is not true is true – so the heart must hastily start doing something, must start expanding as fast as possible.

Expanding inside where it is too cramped already. It is thudding heavily.

But it is still mine.

Spoken somewhere by chance, with a somewhat indefinite purpose. Spoken in defiance.

It is different tonight.

That's what it is. Of course there are other things outside, but it is mine all the same.

It is larger, but it is mine all the same and will remain mine in the future.

This is rank defiance, and it becomes more cramped around my heart that must go on beating. My heart, that has always wanted to expand, is forced instead to feel more cramped than ever when it beats. At the same time wood is thudding against wood outside, and the ring is rattling in the wall.

There are no limits out there. One can imagine distant shores. Great thoroughfares, and harbors in the unknown. Chillingly unknown.

Indoors it thuds against its narrow walls. My heart is too large for its chamber. It is getting feverish in there.

Is this a hand of iron gripping it?

Don't let's talk about that.

The space has suddenly grown larger, not from generosity, but from surprise, and from strenuous expansion in order to find room for all the half forgotten things suddenly remembered and scraped together, in the desire to include them. Suddenly it all comes alive and streams to the heart. Life streams to the heart bearing things that scarcely have names, that have now become important.

For unknown reasons?

No.

The heart is at the roadside; there is no other place to be. It is late, and one must go out naked.

This is not unexpected; preparations were made long ago. Yet it has come too quickly and too soon.

The prow of the boat is butting into the wall, butting into the house, and time is no more than a narrow line at what seems to be the point of exit. Outside the rainstorm has begun. The lonely boat, the rain and the storm; it is hurled against the wall and he who must go out naked discards garment after garment and hears it all as a stern, many-colored song about the brief time and the brief time. The boat is slung about in the rushing and roaring in the brief time. The boat that did not exist, on the ocean that did not exist, and the rushing and roaring around the brief time. This song cannot last, but is lasting now, since the post is tied to the house, and the house is tied to the post, and the ring is inexorably tied to the heart in wind and rain and storm.

The heart is tied in the space which is steadily becoming more cramped because everything is trying to enter it in desperation. From the thoroughfares back in the twilight, from all its ages, from all its defeats and joys, and its shame. Continually in from the thoroughfares, which were always so many, and the wind and the rain over and over again, all of it rushing and roaring through my heart like a song.

Who will shake off what tries to force its way in, and deny it, saying: Here is no flood and no sea-storm, here is no ocean with unknown fairways, here no boat is being made ready for a journey, for night is night and it will be day tomorrow? No, it is too late to sing thus. It is all resolved; the ring is fastened to the wall, the boat is tugging at the ring, late to sing thus.

THE FIRST IRON GRIP is imminent. The iron hand is exerting its grip. Iron is iron, but it is too late to sing thus, when the hand is raised to grip, when the heart is lying at the roadside and is too large and too cramped. Too late the heart understands that it is now, and the dark river is flowing, and the iron hand is exerting its grip.

THE WIND AND THE BOAT are tugging at each other. The wide way of the wind is free; it comes from the unknown, goes to the unknown. Free.

The boat jerks at the rope. The shocked house is a part of the shocked heart, and the thoroughfare to it lay open; the boat is butting impatiently into the door-frame. The house is only a resting place beside the highway. What can the heart do? It is innocent.

Desperate excuses.

The heart is not innocent. How can it be? It is feverish, not innocent. It has shared a man's life. Anything but innocent.

But it is all that streams back, demanding room. The heart cannot deny it room; it must receive it, must expand. It cannot shut it out, nothing is closed tonight, it is fantasy that such and such can be shut out. On the contrary, it must remain open to everything that wishes to come in. No one will ask for permission, never has anything so wretched been done that it cannot come and demand room. Receive, expand. Incredible how much one thought had been buried.

Is *that* coming too?

Yes.

And that too?

Yes.

Like that all the time.

Room must be found, but the walls cannot expand more than they have already. The heart withers in weariness. No more must come.

It speaks like an innocent heart.

It speaks to the storm and the darkness and to that which is nameless and that which cannot be named. Speaks unavailingly of its futile excuses. The iron hands are about to seize it.

The wind has brought heavier rain. Outside a wild rushing and roaring mounts up, inside there is an equally wild rushing and roaring from all these things. Meanwhile the boat thuds, reminding one that it is there, but the rhythm is slower now than it was at first – for the sake of understanding.

And a breathing space between the iron hands, merely for the sake of understanding.

THE WIND BLOWS the downpour forward, as is right and proper on earth. At first it has a calming effect. One can imagine the rain pounding into the empty boat, soaking and blackening the thwarts. Blackening them in the darkness, as if it must be doubly dark. But the wind has blown forward twisted memories too – while it tosses the boat, while the thwarts blacken. Memories fly in frightened flocks.

The pelting rain is streaming down, striking the floorboards. The rope hardens at its mooring.

Familiar and homely. A little breathing space.

If only the heart could shut itself off. It may not do so, and becomes crammed with memories, heavy with images, saving itself by clinging to straws, like the mooring rope and the slight, familiar smell of the mooring rope in rain. The reassuring smell of the commonplace.

A breathing space between iron hands. Soon they will be here. One must cling to the most ordinary things. Nothing is going to happen, do you notice the smell of the mooring rope soaked with rain? Blessedly ordinary.

As calm and normal,

as when ropes are smelling in rain.

NO USE ANY LONGER. The strain on the heart becomes greater. The wind has blown forward something nobody wanted. The dull rhythm out there becomes more insistent, turning to heavier thuds against the wall. One thing is clear: the boat is to stay beside the house. Blackening thwarts or no, it is to wait here.

What then?

It's simply to wait here.

No one shall sing about it.

But no one has any reason to weep either. Is the one perhaps just as simple as the other? It is only that it does not seem so.

Think it over.

I can't.

It was dark to start with, the clouds and the downpour came later. It will not become denser than this. More room is needed, but the iron walls cannot permit it. Soon it will be more cramped. The boat gives constant reminders that it is there, if that means anything. The lonely thwarts and the rain and the wind are dancing with one another in the dense night.

What is happening out there?

It is no dream, it is now. The moment now.

The moment one knew about, and which gave warning of its coming, warning of an arduous and wearisome night.

THE RAIN IS SLANTING low before the storm. The old, unpainted wooden walls out there are already blackened by the driving rain. It does not show, and means nothing at all; it is correct that my house is black.

Yes, old house walls and driving rain – let that find room. The commonplace, and soaked house walls, that's how it should be, in a song. Even if it was formerly a torment, now it is blessed to have the memory of it. To have it in the center of one's heart like love. Once there was love, once there was a frosty night, and spring. The house stands in the night and is dark. A girl who stood in the driving rain and is dead, what of her? My heart expands, but receives nothing. It is large and shocked by memories.

The fine things that were lost have their place in eternity, but eternity somehow seems to be for others.

Large and shocked by memories. Almost forgetting that

there is no room, and reminded of it by iron hands. My heart struggles wildly to escape.

And what is this?

Straight through what is devastating it and filling it up. The dark current is lifting. One is in the iron hands, and the gift of a new eye enables one to see that the current outside is lifting.

Walls are of no consequence. In the congestion a new eye springs out. One knows this and sees it at the same moment. Straight through all obstacles one sees the darker part of the darkness lifting against the wind.

No one could have foretold this. It is lifting against the storm. The boat thuds heavily meanwhile. Something heavy as lead has risen from the bottom in the storm. What does it want? What is it?

The heart is between iron walls, no more must happen now. What is it?

One has an idea of what it is, but will not admit that one understands. The rising of the current was the sign. The dark current will well up and rise like the wind, so that its pale underside shines visible. It will shine in the hour of night above the fairways and the rain-drowned boat and in the fairway of the boat once more. The fairway for the boat must disclose itself even though it has never done so before; it will not be a mystery.

So it is too late to sing now.

The heart grows larger and larger within the walls which have no room; it must break. The current has lifted, and the boat seems to have split its lip against the house, but the storm does not slacken and the thwarts have danced with the rain. All of them are obvious signs that it is too late to sing now.

The current sinks again, but it will soon lift even higher.

ONE KNEW A LITTLE about this uplifting, but did not believe in it. Had an uplifting in oneself that one tried to send out. It was lost. The heart is in distress – so full that *that* is what lifts the current against the storm and the weather, with its naked, white underside.

A NAGGING THOUGHT: I know something all the same.
Oh no.
But I know something all the same.
No! Too late to sing now.

THE CRAMPED CHAMBER with its many old guests. They are thronging back. It is like that when such things happen.
What is happening really?
No answer.
It is a mystery.
That the heart must make itself larger, but cannot. It must break shortly.
The thronging must cease.
The thronging does not cease.
The heart desires the throng, desires everything that used to be, every single thing, the bad and the good, as long as it used to be. The signals are going out now, beckoning in this direction. The throng increases because of it, crowding in. The chamber is bound to break apart soon, but sends

out signals to everyone. The throng presses on, the crush is beyond bearing, since there is no more room, there is no more room, but the throng presses on and the heart sends signals without pause, for a greater throng.

All of that has been forgotten, lost or neglected – it has never really been lost, and now it knows where it came from and where it belongs to. It hears the signal. Does not ask whether there is room. Forces its way in.

The tension is so great that it lifts the current outside into darker ridges. The heart, unable to beat, sends burning impulses through the earth and stone and water. Signals. Desiring to be open to everything, it must clench itself and shrink and wither instead.

But come, come.

Come all that used to be, that belonged here, that went out from here.

The downpour outside seems even heavier. The loose thwarts in the boat may have floated away. Maybe the prow of the boat is completely staved in.

NO CONSIDERATION is shown by those who have been called back. The signal has gone out telling of extreme distress, and here they throng to come in. It is irrelevant that the space is becoming more cramped, it is of no concern that the heart's distress is increasing because of it – when its resting place wishes it to be so.

The beleaguered heart clenches itself and accepts them all.

Choked up, it clenches itself inside the iron ready to break apart.

The signal goes out constantly: Come.

Is there anyone left outside who has not come in? All must come in.

It is night.

This is a struggle.

The signal is sounding in blasts in all the thoroughfares, picking up and bringing back thousands of forgotten details. In spite of torment the ravaged heart cannot cease calling. It will at least send its message. In blinding clarity they will be remembered, sought out and forced back. The heart will never give in; it labours on in a worn-out chamber. Life has been many-faceted and colorful.

Come, come.

This is what life has been like.

Now it is a lonely struggle among memories. The message goes out for more memories. They serve as a weapon. But they make the space increasingly more cramped.

A blind struggle, in diminishing room.

Not blind. The signals deny that.

Processions of them back again. Greater difficulties. Clenching itself to make room.

There must be a breaking point – and now it is almost here. The current from the bottom rises in earnest and the pale underside glimmers through the darkness. It rises higher. The muted glimmer remains. The dark river flows on. On into darkness.

IT BROKE.

Did it break?

No. Not this time.

It only seemed so.

It only felt so in an unbearable moment. On the contrary it broke out into relief. It emerged free of all burdens. All those who were summoned have left.

Ought one to go out as the victor?

No. One cannot do that.

Never as the victor.

But we shall win and we shall not win.

For the time being.

There is a great reserve that stands ready.

One understands this now, knowing they will come as soon as the signals go out. Then one is not lonely, and the hurt takes second place. There are more than many who will volunteer.

FOR THE TIME BEING, as if invincible, the heart lies beside the road to the dark river. Naked, and awaiting the next event, be that what it may.

The Tranquil River Glides Out of the Landscape

WHAT IS STILLNESS LIKE when it is so great that it cannot be grasped? When it has come gliding out of its own place and feels more oppressive than thunder?

It is only someone sailing out of the woods. Not so important, perhaps. Putting himself in order calmly and with strength.

The shining, tranquil river glides out with all its burdens. It comes as if from far away in the interior, and delivers its innermost secrets. On its way towards a distant ocean.

What accompanies it on the journey? Intense desires that have subsided. Nothing more.

The water goes on gliding and gliding.

It does not draw attention to itself. But the land that lies beside it cannot escape being marked by the journey.

Brightly shining water from the innermost core. More shining water follows after. All is tranquil. A tranquil movement that does not look as if it can ever come to an end. Merely moving on. It is all ordered without any trouble.

Large matters and small. And the matter today? What of that?

No matter any longer. This is a farewell procession of quenched, intense desires. And they are being carried to the ocean.

It glides out of the landscape and towards the distant, wide ocean. For the one who has an inkling, however small, of the ocean, the tranquil journey is not important.

THE MIGHTY RIVER casts out what has no resting place. No one interferes with it.

It is as simple as that, as tranquil as that.

AS IF SOMETHING HAS REARED UP behind a hazy hill far beyond what is called the horizon: what has no resting place any longer must be carried away. A river still as a mirror is clear from within; there is no more to it than that, it seems.

The air may be charged with bitter questions, useless questions. They will not be asked. They merely rest above the carrying water, rest while on the move like everything else. No current halts because it is difficult to understand that intense desires are quenched.

The fine carrying surface is filled with reflections from the banks, reflections so vivid that they are ready to tear themselves away and glide with it. But this must be a long journey after all; the hillsides and woods shudder to see their reflections exhibited thus, mirrored so translucently.

The river is the carrier, and it carries away a quenched desire, and has the most limpid water.

Yet the hillsides and woods do not join the company. They see themselves in the water, but remain where they are. It has been ordered so that no one may go wherever he wishes.

QUESTIONS ARE IN THE AIR.

But no answers.

There will never be any answers. The water glides out of the wood and past all questioners. What is so difficult?

Farewell to a thousand glimmers, and a thousand rough raps and noises. What kinds of blessed sounds. What offers resistance? What is reluctant?

None of the banks will collapse; slowly the earth builds up and holds fast, slowly it acquires strength from an incredible variety of sources, and holds.

The shining water and its carrying. It seems so easy. What is difficult to obscure, and shyness forbids further questioning.

This is not exposure to the ravens.

It is high water after gales and heavy rain. Slender birch saplings growing on the banks have not regained their strength after the storm: they stand arched over, dipping their crowns in the water, looking like young girls, gentle, anxious and full of expectancy. The traveller speeds past.

A JOURNEY TO THE OCEAN can scarcely be ordered more fittingly. Gentleness has no part in this. Gentleness is left behind with the pliant birches.

It is difficult to go on?

Not now.

Nothing can be grasped, nothing can be set aside to sink to the bottom. These soundless thunderclaps that are part of the process come first, the mirror of water comes oozing after, obstructed by so many hindrances. Hindrances in the stone walls and the earth banks, in leaning trees, even in bent straws. Imperceptibly it all melts away, it releases the tight little hold it has had. Everything is taken care of, all the grips and holds and hindrances loosen.

Not to be halted by a couple of bent straws.

Not to be halted by a memory.

To have a shining fairway to be carried upon. Now it moves straight on. The surfaces filter through the newest buds the whole time.

It is difficult to go on?

Not now. There's only the final message to be sent out. A slight pause while it becomes clear that we are going to the ocean. But what does that mean?

The answer comes: The ocean is the ocean.

Was that answer good enough? Why did that answer come? Does it perhaps not matter so much any more?

What does good enough mean?

What does matter mean?

No one has said that it does not matter. Have we not heard the thunderclap that this stillness creates? Then it matters enough. Perhaps it did not answer properly after all. It gets more and more difficult to detect an answer. What is it one has not known?

The shining, tranquil water glides out of the landscape, bearing what has no resting place.

Beyond One's Grasp

SCENT OF THE FIRST RAIN on a light dress, over warm flesh.

What of it?

Or on my own light shirt.

Fleeting, precious moments.

A scent that is gone as one turns round and stops speaking. Things that can't last smell like that, things unaware of their existence. Quietly hidden on the tongue behind words of love.

Beyond one's grasp – like the things one would like to have close when one ought not to wish for more.

THE FIRST DROP on a linen shirt.

One stops short on the road and lifts one's face, perceiving something: yet another loss.

A message from a loss, strangely vivid, with no name.

This loss is the final thing of importance, the thing that incites, that strikes, and that creates.

The anticipation is important, but the loss comes last. The road becomes difficult across deep clefts, the side tracks get entangled in their own knots, and the meeting places become invisible.

BUT TO EXPLAIN what is beyond words about the scent of the first rain. There is a truth behind it, a truth one turns away from perhaps.

Again a truth, behind the words of love.

There are layers upon layers. It is wrong to come forward and pretend that one knows.

We sense it as a message, but the signals and the truths conceal themselves behind countless veils. We do not want to know; we accept the scent hastily, before the truth lies naked and near.

Veils. We cover it up quickly. One must keep a sense of wonder – like the longing that rises up between us on warm days, in the first drops in a shower of rain.

THUD, GOES SOMETHING beneath my foot on the ascent, beneath my boot. The flat stone on the path taps gently against the rock when I step on it; it is not lying steady, it can tilt over.

Thud, says the stone.

Not unexpected.

The stone on the path and I are good friends. It has been a reticent friendship for a long time now. Mysterious in its extreme simplicity.

Never disappointing.

A thud today as usual.

Or is it different this year? Once more, slightly new and different?

Why should that be?

Stuff and nonsense, I say, but perhaps I really wished it to be so.

Thud, at any rate, in affirmation, sealing the compact, tilting and tapping on the rock. A signal far within saying that it is now. That it simply is.

What is now? That is not explained. But it speaks to my heart and I understand the language. It speaks softly as if to someone poor and shy.

All's well, it means.

I say nothing about my affairs; it is a soliloquy about our long friendship. All's well.

Thud, about you and me and the summer, the brief summer, our happiness, evenings – and then that subtle signal from within. One imagines that it is being passed along far, far inside in the heavy rock chambers. And there the message is clear.

IT WILL CONTINUE on the steep ascent.

All's well.

The stone with its gentle welcome.

The stone that is there to stay.

The stone will greet each new wanderer on the ascent in its reticent language. Throughout all ages and throughout all ages. The restless wanderer will find peace and yet more peace.

And you?

Shyly you came to the path and asked. Shyly you came to know and understand.

Just Walking Up to Fetch the Churn

IT SEEMS SO TRIVIAL, but it doesn't take much.

Just walking up to fetch the milk churn early one morning can be a miracle.

The scents are a part of it. They are forgotten and reappear, like old songs. The great song about scents cannot be learned by heart, but it accompanies you wherever you go.

THE SUN CAME UP recently over the ridge, and is spilling over the hillside. You have come out of the house to fetch the milk churn from the ledge up by the road. It is summer.

The scents matured during the hot day yesterday. Last night they hovered here acquiring a cool, intoxicating taste, but translucent and a little distant from us too. The sun renews it all in a moment.

And not only renews, but creates for today. Every day something new at this hour. The greenwood quickens as it does in the song, and our own hillsides quicken too. It is all around us, it will never leave us. It is like an agreement about being here together.

There are many things one would not want to miss. Just walking up to the road to fetch the milk churn in this teeming hour, before a new day in the heat-wave.

The hour of becoming before full daylight. He who sleeps sins when he sleeps away this.

FAMILIAR FARMYARD BIRDS fly up from the steps as you leave the house. Magpie and starling. Pretending to be afraid; not afraid at all. Out and about early. They settle on the nearest roof-tree, not the slightest bit scared. Simply looking to see whether anything has been dropped. The swallows are already sweeping the sky in endless pursuit; by evening they must be some of the most exhausted creatures in the world. Who could imagine that of a streamlined, floating swallow! In the morning you find joy, and the swallow itself seems born of blue air and joy.

When you finally reach the main road the newly arrived milk churn is standing on the platform. The lane that leads up to it is a short one and makes a familiar crunching sound. It is on a hillside too. Nothing but hills. All of a sudden you feel the sun on your shoulders like a warm embrace.

The sun-warmed earth with its blades of grass, its ants and its flowers makes the hillside breathe out mixed spices towards you. And mixed for today.

Spices. Beyond all reason it makes you think of the cardamom-scented air in a pre-Christmas house when you were a child. In a snowed-under house in a snowed-under farmyard, a yard glittering with frost. There is no resemblance, but the wonderful enticement grips you, now as then.

Beyond all reason. But it is good. A dizziness at being alive in the midst of everything that makes the earth a fine place to live in. From a rustling summer morning to cardamom.

AND THEN THE GIRL on the road.

She came walking along simply in order to round off the picture. Girls on the road. They belong.

She belongs to the morning, walking long-legged, as if stepping in tall grass – I do not understand why. There is no grass on the crunching road. I cannot ask her, it is simply beautiful and right that she should walk like that, exactly like that. It would have been the same however she moved, I suppose. You can see she is walking wide-eyed because of the morning. Walking home in wonderment. Perhaps she has come from a dance somewhere and is happy. Stepping as if in tall grass.

The birches lean towards each other above the lane as she passes; they meet above her head as if she were a new Bendik's maid.[1] As if in tall grass she walks, not into death, but towards life.

FLOWERS AMONG THE STONES, and buds ready to open. The sun will pour down and the scents change as everything is awakened. You can see it already: never has there been such intense flowering on the hillsides as this year. As there will be, many have not yet blossomed. You are a part of this. You are meant to be here.

1 Bendik and Aurolilja: a medieval Norwegian ballad of doomed love. The flowers planted on the lovers' graves met and entwined overhead.

The strong awareness of being part of it all. In wonderment you walk on the hillside, in a morning shower of strangeness, just to fetch the milk churn.

The Melody

A SHADOW OVER HER?

No, none.

Does he see no shadow on her?

Not now.

There has been no shadow for many years.

No, and the dead cannot rise out of the earth to create one either. So there is none.

THE LIGHT was not always so clear.

During the time when we were in her care and growing up, it could darken a little, and shadows could speed past, and sorrows speed past. They could feel bitter. In fact they were tremendous fantasies. Clear light shines around her. We cannot claim to be able to point to a single stain. Perhaps it has been washed away because we do not want to know about it, cannot bear it, will not allow it.

If anyone says it is not true, we are at once prepared with the answer that it is more than true, unshakeably true. And so it always will be. Do not come and say anything that creates shadows, face to face with such firm faith.

BEAUTIFUL GIRLS.

For a boy there is strong enchantment in the word alone. We heard it and were aware of it for years, without being clear about what it meant. Later we learned how mistakenly, to the point of absurdity, it could be used. How uncertain a judgement it was. How blind and superficial it could be. It was not an easy lesson to learn.

But when we saw it lying thickly outside too, then we could not help ourselves. One was drawn towards it, and wanted to be drawn towards it. What was it? A state of well-being. An uplifting into something light, so it seemed, where one did not really belong, but was graciously allowed to stay for a little. It usually vanished quite quickly and was gone elsewhere.

We listened tensely to this talk of beautiful girls, alongside our own thoughts. We had them for a good and obvious reason.

At home there was an album bound in yellow leather, and in it there were beautiful girls. We often looked at it when the grown-ups were out of the room. But we saw most of them with indifference, we only looked at one of them.

And we saw her alive every single day.

The others in the album were her friends at the school she had attended as a grown girl. They were strangely dressed-up, these girls, in clothes that were different from those we were used to seeing on women. Most of them had piled up their hair, and all of them were smooth and pale, with skin like cream.

We leafed past them until we came to the place we were looking for, to the only important one.

Perhaps she was dressed up too, but no more than was just right. When we came to her in the pages of the album we did not say a word. We had habitual ways of talking about the others, and not particularly flattering ones either, making fun of things that differed too much from the way we thought they should be. *Here* we did nothing like that. We fell silent and looked.

At her.

She was just as she should be.

In every way.

But at the same time we saw something else that surprised us and worried us a little.

This was how Mother had looked when she was a girl and utterly young. So exciting and so attractive. And so kind in every way, it seemed. And so incredibly soft – and we weren't thinking about cream.

Yes, but there was something in all this that was never mentioned. We did not wish to. We just thought it. We could hear her as we sat there thinking. She was as close as that, working on the other side of the door, clattering pots and kettles and pans, dishes and washing-up – there would be many workers to feed that day as usual. If she came as far as the door to keep an eye on the youngest her face was warm and perspiring; the day was hot beside the cooking stove.

We sat with her beautiful album, and without a word, in the greatest secrecy, we quietly compared the girl in the album with the woman of today with the pots and perspiration and one thing and another, that had at least begun to worry the eldest of us.

For they were not exactly alike, these two girls who ought to have been so. The comparison told us this clearly enough. We looked, and kept silent.

We looked at the photograph of the very young, vivacious girl for a long time and tried to discover how much of what we saw was still there. We discovered a good deal of it too. We were clever enough to see that. It's about the same, we probably told ourselves. We did not understand the new values that had been added, and more than weighed up those that had gone. Occasionally the eldest, who had the responsibility, would exclaim "She *is* kind!" in an angry tone of voice.

The younger ones sat with unaltered expressions.

One had to cling to the page in the album, to the gentle young girl there.

If we looked at the pictures together with people from outside the farm, we would point quickly and indifferently, informing with the outermost finger tip: "Mother." Then leaf quickly on.

"No, wait," the outsider might say and leaf back. Then we would all look at her for a long time, and we were tense.

"Indeed!" they said to us small boys. "Indeed!"

A hint of what they put into that annoying "Indeed!" must have struck us. Surely they could have kept their mouths shut, they as well as other people?

⌒

IMMERSED IN THAT MELODY.

What was it exactly?

Something we had at home and did not understand.

Outwardly it was the simple plucking that we did not

pay much attention to, we who were born without much appreciation of music.

Early winter darkness out of doors. An early winter's night, a long time until bedtime.

It was snowing out of doors. Snow, snow the whole day long, snow floating down invisibly and incessantly. We had no outside lamp.

The living-room window pane squinted indifferently out into the snowstorm. The lamp indoors cared nothing for snowstorms and difficult walking conditions and unploughed, snowed-up roads. The oil lamp indoors burned, muted and cozy.

But someone was going out tonight, in spite of the weather. Out to the music. Snow had never yet shut her out from the music that sang inside her.

Under the lamp she is practicing her alto melody, plucking at a long wooden, stringed instrument, plucking through her homework. She will take the melody with her out into the snow and the darkness, her skis dragging heavy on her feet.

Determined to reach the others with her melody this evening.

We listen and we know this. We think it strange that she should want to go out in such weather.

Her husband says, "Are you going out this evening?"

She does not understand. She is filled with the melody.

"Of course, why not? We're going to sing."

"Yes, yes," he says.

He is lying over on the bed with a book in his hand, the tall master of the house. It is not a strenuous time of year; on the contrary there are long evenings when you can enjoy yourself with a book. It is possible to read, you are not too tired. And you have the energy to share the music, if you understand it. We are aware of how much better it is to be alive in the dark, cold winter snow, than in the busy summer with an aching body.

He has read many books aloud to us, that severe man over there on the bed. To our great delight. But this evening he is reading to himself, since the melody is plinking.

He has not finished with the subject of going out into the tiring snow.

"In this weather?" he says.

"It would have to be very bad," she replies quickly.

She is immersed in the melody. The rest of us do not know what it means. The man with the book cannot imagine it either. He is like his sons. There is a slight edge to his voice as he continues, "Well, I can't make it out."

She tumbles out of the melody and says bitterly, "I know you can't."

"No, I think one ought to rest when one has the chance."

He cannot be so very tired this evening, surely. But he always has a bad back to plague him and set limits.

"It's no use, whatever you say," she tells him and puts an end to the little quarrel.

Silence in the living-room. The melody has been shattered. The maid sits as if she did not exist at such moments. The rest of us, little as well as half grown, have heard similar exchanges many times. The eldest thinks, as so often before: What's the matter with them?

It shouldn't be like this.

Will he go with her? No.

We understand what the talk is really skirting: the snowed-up road to the village. The man does not consider he can face going out into the storm to make a ski track over to the music. It is probably true that he is tired out and ought to rest his back. Over to the music – it's not a matter of life and death to get there.

He clears his throat.

Is there more? We wait.

"Well, well," is all he says. It sounds like a kind of announcement of his intention to stay where he is.

He takes up his book with a jerk, a favorite book that he has read many times. The plucking on the string has started again too.

SHE GOES OUT into the chaos of snow, accompanied by the melody.

The melody is all about her. The melody must never, never leave her.

We are left sitting, but in a way we accompany her too.

We are not afraid of anything happening to her. She has skis on her feet, and she is a good skier and accustomed to using them. The yellow album was given to her as a ski prize once. Everyone knows she will manage to get there in spite of the bad weather. And yet....

Brush it aside.

The melody goes before her in the darkness too.

A strange thought, but you can see it clearly. Both of them are out there together.

We glance at the tired, silent master of the house with his books. He has put the book down and is staring at something on the ceiling.

He is uncomfortable.

We can see that. You learn to know the faces you have in front of you every single day. We are careful about what we say and do not say now.

After a while he coughs, swings himself off the bed, slips into his boots, and goes out.

Did he go after her? What a relief!

No. He comes back in again at once. He has not put on his outdoor clothes either. We do not notice that in our initial astonishment.

"Is it just as nasty outside?"

The youngest asking in all innocence. His father answers quickly, "Nasty? Have I said it's nasty? Oh no, I've seen much worse."

He looks searchingly at the child, takes off his boots and stretches out full length on the bed, letting the book lie.

Go out after her? Oh no, he's too stiff-necked to do that, the eldest one has learnt. It would have cost far too much to follow her, to overtake her and make a ski-track over that comparatively short distance.

But what is it that comes over them sometimes?

Easy to see her now: with the plinking melody for company, making her way through the drifts, steadily and surely. Over to the house with the many lamps and all the melodies. He sees her like this too, the man with the closed book.

One understands a little more each day. But there is a dark core that one cannot crack – and that's where the answer to the puzzle lies.

We can only see her, simply and straightforwardly, making her way through the drifts. She arrives safely at her meeting with the melody. She goes in and is received with unreserved happiness. And now she is happy herself. And then we know nothing more until we see her again tomorrow morning.

Then she is back in place, serving us food. Food for us everlastingly, morning, noon and night. By the time she came home yesterday evening we were sleeping bundles, sailing in dreams above bottomless whirlpools.

DID I SAY SIMPLY?

Years later one thinks about such evenings, and sees her in the storm. No, not simply.

The hidden thing that is the melody is about her: the man she is bound to; the children who have sprung from her womb; the hard, rigorous law that pulsates in the darkness together with the melody, the law about carrying out the duties one has taken upon oneself – all this is part of it too. She is in the middle of it all, forced by life.

Someone like her, having made a promise, would probably never go back on it, as long as she had the strength.

Her skis must be sinking deep into the new snow. She certainly won't let it bother her. She has gone that way so many times that she doesn't even see it. She is going to a brightly-lit room with music and friends filled with music. She will come as a bonus to their happiness, bringing her own alto melody with her.

Those left at home cannot go with her, but she insists on having the music there. It shall be there as long as I am there in that house. My house shall be a house where there is room for the music too.

This is probably what she is thinking as she moves along in the storm.

I shall win him over, she must be thinking. I shall not give up, she must be thinking. I shall leave my mark on my home. Are we too dissimilar? perhaps she is thinking.

If he had gone too and cleared a track for her she would have been immensely happy and immensely embarrassed. Perhaps mostly embarrassed.

⟶

THERE WERE MANY TREES in the farmyard. Splendid trees had stood there when the eldest was a little boy.

When he was a little boy and could say out loud like an easy wish: Wind in my trees. Although he did not use those words exactly.

There was wind enough. The mass of leaves on the big aspen quivered and the many rowans fanned and combed the air on nights when the wind blew strong. Beside the red wall of the loft stood a bird-cherry tree, and at times the heavy scent of the blossom came in through the little round window.

Inside lay the boy in his lonely resting place, usually dead tired. He thought of the fragrance as part of his wild dream, because it never came true.

Nothing was going to fly apart; it only felt as if it might.

But it shall fly apart all the same, it shall happen, someone shall come, it shall arrive like some kind of miracle before everything is over.

The walls of old summer lofts have an odor of gently disturbing dreams that never came to anything. Now yet another naked boy was lying there in the hot weather, staring at the roof, lacking certainty. Yet another boy in the series. The roof that was dark and therefore endless, and not really there at all.

Lying there with his too-young years, thinking about everything that he was not allowed to think about, and not allowed to talk about.

ROOFS LIFT OFF HOUSES on such summer nights, and you can see what is inside. In the attic bedroom beside the loft lie two young girls, brought in by Mother to rake the hay now it is the busy season. The roof lifts off the house and the boy sees them lying there and lying there, but he is not old enough to go in and fool around with them. But others go there. Many late evenings and nights of joking and talk on the other side of the wall. Lively talk and laughter, and soft, intimate talk. For a short while before everyone gets up there is silence. Only the wind whispers in the aspen.

Day breaks. The mistress of the house comes out into the yard and calls to them to get up. Tells them that it is morning. The girls come out, narrowing their eyes against the light, and Mother, who was the first to be out in the whispering-leaved yard, gives them their breakfast.

The boy from the loft looks at the two girls a little shyly and curiously. Are they different today?

They must be different, or nothing makes sense at all. They must be renewed or something, after a night full of marvels. Perhaps they are not, after all?

Is there no mark on them, only those narrowed eyes? Nothing else.

They walk along with their fine legs and everything else that a young boy cannot help noticing and delighting in and thinking about. But they act as if they were indifferent, and look it too.

Their narrowed eyes are happy, to be sure, but so they were before. Mother says that the two of them are so good-natured and pleasant to have around. The boy thinks to himself that one might well be happy, if one had nights like theirs.

But instead their luster is a little dimmed today. They are not golden, as one might expect.

Such a thing makes you thoughtful. It has to be hidden away, along with other secret matters.

THE NEW DAY has been set in motion. The mowers come out. He looks at them for a long time. Wasn't there a familiar voice in the attic bedroom last night? Have they slept or have they only gone to bed?

And was this in any way important?

In one way. A door was starting to open on to something new. He would have to pay attention to a lot of things, if he were to find some meaning in it.

But something quite different gave the day its particular stamp: the erect, slightly-built woman who had inaugurated it. She it was who stood first in the yard, and who had to remain on her feet until late at night. Her hands and her thoughts were essential wherever something had to be done. And in the busy season something was happening everywhere.

No one giggled behind her back. Nor did she ever have a disparaging word for any of her workfolk.

They might grimace at the farmer instead – even though he was well thought-of really, and tactful. The eldest boy watched him and did not understand him. This man was fond of songs too, and after the meal breaks, when they sat beside the grindstone, the hired men often sang, and the man who could not sing recited songs and discussed songs, and knew more about them than anyone. It was impossible to make him out.

But you could not approach him and ask for advice about all that gnawed at your heart. Never. Nor did the man ever refer to what was gnawing inside him.

He was liked, although he could make people extremely irritated at times. No doubt about it, he was liked.

"Well, girls?" he said today, smiling at them. "Was it hard to get up?"

The boy was not the only one to have heard the racket in the night, evidently.

He smiled at them. They smiled confidently back without replying. They were not in the least afraid of him.

His wife would not have done that. They would have flushed red if she has made the slightest reference to what went on in the attic bedroom.

⌣

THE CRUEL SUMMER is inescapable: it belongs with life on the farm.

The eldest watches her. You ought not to be working like this, Mother, he thinks constantly. This isn't what you ought to be doing.

Strange girl in the album.

But haymaking is haymaking, and no way of avoiding it. They must have made an agreement.

The pleasant morning dew must be turned to account.

Sharp-edged scythes slither in cold morning dew, and bite twice as keenly. Up with the dawn for that reason. The girls too. They are turning the piles of hay.

She is not out yet. First the house and the children, and the food that must soon be ready on the table again. But afterwards: raking the haycocks, turning the windrow, cooking dinner, raking up the dried hay after the wagon has gone jolting past.

This isn't what you ought to be doing, Mother.

Nonsense. No use talking like that. This is why we're here.

The sweat runs. Backs stiffen. And the stiffest back belongs to the master of the farm who injured it in his youth, logging in the woods.

The imperious fine weather hounds us on mercilessly. Perhaps you secretly long for a little shower, a little welcome, relaxing rain. You must not say so. Haymaking weather is important; you ought to be giving thanks for it.

But Mother must not wear herself out so. Don't you see that it's too hard?

He would like to be able to seize the tanned thin man

and shake him and say so that he would understand: Don't you see?

No one sees. It's quite all right.

Does she think it's all right to be worn out like this?

It looks like it, that's what's so extraordinary. What kind of promise has she made?

He watches the book fall from her hands in the evening after the house has been made ready. He sees his father lying on his bed, dozing over a book. From pure exhaustion. This is not as it should be.

The beautiful girls on the haying strip discard some of their clothes and there is even more to look at. Things that you're not supposed to see, so that it startles you. The mowers' eyes are gentle far into the day. But in the evening everything is snuffed out and tired and sleeping and gone. Isn't it a shame?

Mother, who bears the brunt indoors, slouches from exhaustion and will be the last to go to bed. Isn't it a shame? Is it as it should be?

Her son looks at her and thinks: Did she know this the day she promised to come here and live with him?

Of course she did. She must have seen it during her own youth. She knew what she was going to.

She must regret it horribly now.

It doesn't look like that, either. And after all, she has us—

Stop now.

SHE SITS WITH ONE CHILD beside her and one on her arm, looking as if everything is really all right. The man who is their father goes over to them, bringing all his unattractive, made-up pet names for them. He has many of them and invents new ones all the time. They sit together for a while, and the eldest hangs about close by, drawing nearer in case he can catch something of what they are saying at such a happy moment.

He is terrified that they will part without saying anything besides the pet names he has for the children.

She says: "You really ought to rest your back sometimes. This will never do."

He answers curtly: "*That* would certainly never do."

HE KNEW what she thought about awkward matters. Those embarrassed and shrinking matters that one never brought oneself to mention. As he grew, his thoughts circled around her more and more nearly, but it was difficult to come close to her. Never really close. But she had said of the awkward matters: "I believe there is something behind, guiding it all, and we must not forget that it is so."

She had said this in several ways. We were never in any doubt about what she believed.

But she never made us embarrassed and awkward by asking intimate questions. We were all silently grateful to her for it, from the bottom of our hearts. Her affairs were her own, and ours were our own too.

We too had our thoughts about such matters. And so we walked beside her just as confidently as when we walked beside the giggling girls who were thinking about boys. Well, who knows about that, anyway? They must have thought about other things beside boys; maybe they sometimes thought about the same things as Mother did. One had to keep it to oneself.

The secret was: we were glad that someone thought the way Mother did. But for pity's sake no questioning and prying.

SUNDAY ALONE with her in the living-room. Late summer and fine weather. The killing hay-making weather could continue fine into the autumn, now that there was a brief pause between harvests. Sunday was no longer just a doze before Monday.

The younger ones had gone with their father to the woods. He had actually asked them whether they would come with him for a short walk.

Grinning with happiness they had accompanied him. She remained sitting in the living-room with the eldest.

The girls were elsewhere, everyone was elsewhere. But one sat contentedly here with Mother. Nothing would happen. Nor could he broach his own worries, however urgent they seemed to him. It was absurd, but that's how he was.

She had a new melody to learn and was plinking through it repeatedly.

He watched her covertly as she did so. He saw what he had seen before: the same as he had seen in the girl in the yellow album, he was sure of it. Now she was at home in the music, and was the girl from the album. Streaks of relief went through him when he saw it.

He sat as still as a mouse. No one may come now, no one may come tramping in here. This must not be destroyed by good days and boring Sunday chat.

She ran through her melody a couple of times more.

THIS EVENING she would be meeting the others, where she somehow seemed to belong.

Or was it not so? Did she belong here all the same? If only she did. Had she found her rightful place, or had a sin been committed? He couldn't make it out.

She was extremely efficient in her present position. She knew her duty, out and in. And more than her duty. She was the mistress here and behaved as if she were.

But at this moment she was the beautiful girl from the album, who had grown and changed, but was still the same. It was the first time he had seen it clearly.

She laid the instrument aside, and came over to him. Right up to him.

At once he was flustered. Had he been mistaken? Did she want something since they were so completely alone? As long as it wasn't about these awkward matters.

He squirmed. Was she going to spoil this happy time? It must be something unusual.

She said, "You're so big now, that there's something I want to tell you."

"There's no need to be nervous," she added, when he started noticeably.

Out with it then, he wished. Don't torture me.

"There are one or two things I want to tell you about us girls," she said calmly. "So that you needn't go worrying yourself about all the nonsense you may hear."

This made him even more flustered, but for different reasons now. She had a teasing expression in her eyes. She said, "You're beginning to take notice of them."

"Am I?"

"You know you are."

Yes, he thought. I know I am.

And then she told him about girls, and about their periods, and about boys. Some of it he knew already and a good deal of it he did not know.

Finally she said, "I sent the others out, so that we would be on our own."

He had never experienced so strange a Sunday in all his life.

⌒

AFTER THAT DAY there was a new bond between them. But it could not be an entirely uninhibited one. Indeed, it never became so. There was a hidden obstacle in him that he could not surmount. On her side there would certainly have been nothing in the way.

A black autumn evening.

Late. One after the other they went to bed. The master of the house was not at home. Finally only two of them were left. They sat waiting for the traveller's return.

Everything was silent. There was a smell of rotten leaves

and grass around the house. And then the waiting for someone who ought to have come home, but had not. He had gone to the neighboring district that morning, to meet someone. He had many acquaintances round about, especially among people who were fond of horses.

Now the two of them were sitting waiting. She must have noticed that he had no intention of going to bed, but was simply finding something to do in order to stay with her.

Without looking up from her book, she said, "Go to bed now."

"I can stay up a bit longer, can't I?"

"You'd best go to bed, do you hear?"

He understood very well why. She wanted him out of the way. He was not to be an observer, in case all was not as it should be when his father came home. This might happen at long, long intervals, not as often as twice a year, even. But that was what she was so absurdly afraid of, beyond everything else. She was crushed by it.

"Why?" he asked, knowing the reason perfectly well.

"Oh—"

"I want to see too," he said, in unexpected defiance.

She reddened, and put down her book. He had gone too far, but was not going to turn back now.

"I know what it is, you see," he said again, "so why shouldn't I stay?"

She rose and came across to him.

"You're to go. This is my affair. You haven't the slightest idea what we're talking about. It's between me and him. You have no part in it."

Unsettling words. He went to his room at once. His younger brother was lying asleep, his mouth wide open.

BEFORE THE MAN SET OUT that morning he had been in great good humour. It was a holiday for everyone and he had been lying on the bench where he rested, chatting and telling them about the Khirgiz steppes and the herds of horses there. Not a new topic for him. The Khirgiz steppes was his pipe dream. Through purposeful reading he had collected a good deal of knowledge about that part of the world. To him it must have been the land of heart's desire.

We always enjoyed listening when he described it. It was a tale told with love, and therefore remembered long.

Then he had harnessed his horse this morning and driven to see his friends.

What sort of company was he keeping now, instead of coming home? It obviously had something to do with horses and old friends. No more dangerous than that. But this touched a fiercely sensitive spot in the girl from the album. There she sat waiting. Her mood immediately transferred itself to him, turning into deep anxiety. It linked up with other matters that were not going to be explained. They never would be. A matter so private that it could not even be passed on to the children.

Sleep now.

No. Lying awake, listening for sounds from the living room. We're sure to hear the sound of cartwheels soon.

After all, there's nothing extraordinary about coming home from a party. From the companionship of good friends who understand about the Khirgiz steppes and that sort of thing. Who like hearing about the enormous steppes and the beautiful horses. He's probably telling them all about it.

May he not come home in party mood after such an evening? A little to drink and the Khirgiz steppes.

She's fond of parties herself. That's where there's music. She can go to parties and dances herself, and take part in the dancing – as long as the melody is there. And she comes home afterwards, walking on air. May he not come from *his* dreams occasionally, a little happier than usual?

No, there's something I've not been told. Something the two of them keep strictly to themselves. It must be more serious than it looks. I'll never dare ask about it. I'd rather not know.

STILL NO WAGON in the yard. Silence in the house.

She's sitting with her book. Or perhaps with a different one.

Both of them sit reading whenever they have time to spare. They have a good point of contact there. They talk about books they have read. One listens to them thirstily. If there had been no books, what then? In this household the books seem heaven-sent.

Could there have been an accident? A serious accident? And we have no telephone. The thought of an accident gives him the excuse to creep in to her.

She starts up, book in hand.

"Oh, it's you! What do you want?"

"Could something have happened?" he stammers.

"No, of course not. They're enjoying themselves, I expect, and time passes as usual."

"Why don't you go to bed too, Mother?"

"Yes, I think I will after all. I can't sit up any longer."

She looks drained and thoroughly exhausted. His old thoughts return.

"Shall I go out and look?" he asks.

"What good will that do? Nothing will have happened near here."

She must have noticed that it sounded a little odd, and smooths it over with a yes, yes, of course something could happen right outside.

At that moment the sound of cartwheels is heard. They both start in surprise. She says hastily, "Go back to your room. Can't you do as I ask? He's not to see that you're sitting up too, waiting for him like this. He wouldn't put up with it. That's why, don't you see?"

Of course. He seems to understand. He must remember that she has brought him into the world. Borne him and reared him. He is back in bed in a couple of strides. He is not going to witness any sort of humiliation of either of them. He can see that she is extremely frightened.

He does not snuggle down in bed and draw the blanket up round his ears. Far from it. He has to listen in case he hears anything that might throw light into the darkness, although he is afraid of what it might be.

Now he can hear the wheels crunching in the gravel out in the yard. They stop.

Oh, how he feels for her! He buries himself at the bottom of the bed.

No, he must listen.

He hears her go out of the living-room to meet her

husband. The yard is black as pitch, no use peeping through the window. But he dare not get dressed and go out into the darkness. They might catch sight of him, and she did ask him to go away.

He hears their voices out there, alternating in ordinary conversation. Is the newcomer raising his voice too much? Don't know.

He is secretly listening for the sound of weeping. That did happen once. Only once, but that was enough; it sticks in the memory as if nailed there.

He can hear nothing of the sort now. She must have been worrying needlessly?

The horse has to be looked after. They are gone from the yard for a long while. What are they doing all this time? No, it isn't a long time really.

But then he hears them. They are coming from the stable towards the house. They are talking eagerly. Both of them raising their voices. Both of them happy and light-hearted.

Light-hearted?

Yes. No reluctant words can be distinguished. No, no.

ENTHUSIASTIC TALK, nothing more. Strong and clear, that draws you into it. He is telling her something, and the words pour out, and she is drawn into it. You can hear her laughter, as if she herself were on the Khirgiz steppes tonight, on a flying horse.

The Rivers Beneath the Earth

NIGHT AS WELL AS DAY.

One is in one's secret chamber, feeling this: Is not the ground quivering beneath my feet, because of the hidden waters?

And what should one do then? I wonder.

One must be present.

One must come forward and stand in the current flowing from them. One must let the faint quivering jolt one. As decaying bridges and old duckboards quiver slightly in the time of the thaw.

OR IN THE DISTANT TIME of youth, when the quivering was within oneself in the form of endless questioning. When one was so terrified oneself of being questioned.

Do I understand more now?

No. But I quiver less.

One is just as wordless in the face of the great riddles, and one still hopes one will not be asked.

But at least to have a place where there is no need to hide, where one simply says: I can hear. I exist, and I can hear the current flowing.

One can be deluded into saying: I exist for the sake of the rivers beneath the earth.

To listen and understand.

Not to understand, but to be as close to where it is happening.

Not to try to understand the enormous network beneath the earth. Where lakes multiply into countless sources, which again multiply into countless sources and finally into unimaginably small sources. Source upon source – while the thirsty stand thirsty behind the thirsty.

When one has understood this, and yet not understood, what is one to do?

The current never stops. As a great pulse never stops.

IT WILL ALWAYS BE NIGHT. It does not make so much difference any more. One hears, all through the night. The alien pulse is laboring close by.

Afraid? No. A little numbed, yet uplifted.

Since it is close by, one understands that the walls have no significance. Numbed and uplifted one cannot help but notice how the pulse beats closer when it is night and the walls are gone.

The swift current is about to return. One meets it flowing back.

How is that?

The pulse in the night may chase sleep away, but the memories are not lost or destroyed. One listens for what one does not understand, as always.

THAT'S WHAT THE NIGHT IS FOR. Different, but not hostile. The currents go cascading back.

What of it?

All's well.

THE NIGHT OPENS its clear vault, and one's eyes open theirs. In the night all eyes are large and wide open, dark to the very edge.